SKIN PRAYER

(Fragments of Abject Memory)

by

Doug Rice

ERASERHEAD PRESS

The Avant-Pop Series

Acknowledgments:

Some of these works have appeared in different forms in the following: *Discourse, Fiction International, Lethologica, Journal of Narrativity, Undershorts Magazine, Trepan, Tough Guys, Hard Code,* and *Morbid Curiosity.* Parts of *Skin Prayer* have been plagiarized, borrowed, stolen, reimagined from *A Good Cuntboy is Hard to Find.*

ISBN: 0-9713572-7-7

Eraserhead Press
16455 E. Fairlynn Dr,
Fountain Hills, AZ 85268
email: publisher@eraserheadpress.com
website: www.eraserheadpress.com

For my children:

Cory Douglas
Anna Livia
Quentin Joyce

A special thank you to Jack Jamieson and Bob Meindl for their deep friendship and saving graces. They change the way I think and open doors I never knew existed.

My way of speaking into the world would not have been possible without the guidance of incredible and passionate teachers and friends: Bonnie Birch, Colin MacCabe, Jamie Snead, Lidia Yuknavitch, Laurie Weeks, Ed Kopper, Paul Bove, Marcia Landy, Philip Smith, Jim Knapp, Suzette Henke, John C. Gardner, Bernie Freydberg, Steven Shaviro, Jalal Toufic, Jasmine Sailing, Amanda Godley, Mark Hennelly, David Matlin, Ben Lybarger, Gary Carlson, Dan Watkins, Craig Paulenich, John A. Clair, and Raymond Federman. I have been blessed.

To Heaven Gainsbrugh.

The following is a work of fiction.
You have to live it everyday, Bruce.

Let me inside you
Into your room
I've heard it's lined
With things you don't show
—Chrissie Hynde

I gave you my skin
And my original sin
—Melissa Etheridge

Contents

Section Three: A Series Of Followings

Afterword: Born To Ruin By Larry McCaffery

By Way Introduction: An Informal Email Exchange Between Alejandro Espinoza (Spanish Translator Of Doug Rice's Work) And Don Harrold (Rice's Primary Editor)

DEAR DON: I'LL BE SORT OF DIALOGUING ALONG WITH YOUR COMMENTS, SO AS TO ESTABLISH SOME FORM OF CONVERSATION ON YOUR THOUGHTS ABOUT MY INQUIRIES. (OBVIOUSLY, MY PART WILL BE WRITTEN IN CAPITAL LETTERS)
Alejandro

d harrold wrote:
> let's see if I can make any sense of these notes.
> went over your email several times and wrote things
> in the margin, then didn't have time to rewrite in
> any kind of order. wanted to get something to you
> asap, so here they are. i'll hope to expand, and
> maybe you'll need to ask what the hell i meant in
> places. i also apologize for not being able to
answer in spanish.

Alejandro: BY THE WAY, ARE YOU ABLE TO READ IN SPANISH? I THINK IT WILL BE A NICE START IF I SHOWED YOU SOME OF THE TRANSLATED WORK.

Don Harrold: all translations of writers who are any good always carry something that cannot be said, but which is that writer. for me, the primary thing in doug rice's writing is energy—he gives off energy. Most people, let alone writers, are either neutral or only take energy. if you can capture that energy-giving essence, you have done your job.

Alejandro: I THINK THE ENERGY COMES FROM THE FACT THAT HIS SENTENCES PORTRAY A SERIES OF ACTIVE IMAGES, A RITUAL BODY MOVEMENT IS CONSTANTLY AT STAKE, WHICH MAKES THE READER MORE OF AN ACTIVE WITNESS, RATHER THAN A SIMPLE CONTEMPLATIVE SUBJECT. AT SOME POINT, THE READER BECOMES THE IMAGE. THE READER BECOMES THE TEXT. IT MIGHT SOUND KOOKY, BUT I THINK IT'S TRUE.

Don: but let me get to things in your email.
"sort of like catching something in mid-sentence,
and it is a narrative of action." what you are
seeing in that "mid-sentence" idea is actually part
of one of rice's repetoire [sic?] of sentence
patterns that you could use
TRUE. NEVER THOUGHT OF THAT.

you could try building such a collection of sentence patterns, an
equivalent, not the same as the english. for
example, "Cruel is this coming to blood. To her
blood." [and this could go on in a series of "To..."
etc] most of the time, these are echoes of something
said, one clear sentence, then a trailing off. this
is just one technique he uses that you could carry
over. i have a hard time calling anything doug
writes "narrative."
TRUE ALSO, I USED IT FOR LACK OF A BETTER WORD

AT THE MOMENT I WROTE THE MESSAGE

It all seems some kind of monolog of a poet trapped at the base of language.

IT IS A MONOLOG, AND IT ALSO IS A FORM OF PRAYER, A VERY SEDUCTIVE, VEY INTIMATE PRAYER, THAT COMES (I THINK) FROM DOUG'S IMMERSION IN THE WORKS OF THE SAINTS. I TOLD HIM THAT SOMETIMES HIS WRITING REMINDS ME OF ST. AUGUSTINE. THAT'S WHEN I FOUND OUT ABOUT ST. THERESA, WHOSE WORK I'VE NEVER BEEN ABLE TO FIND.

"action" is correct. [i think rice gets off on adjectives sometimes, and i try to save him from that. i suggest that you cut as many adjectives as possible when translating

I'M DOING THAT

—that might help with sentence length.

LENGTH, AND ALSO THE FACT THAT, ONCE I START TRANSFORMING DOUG INTO SPANISH, HIS SENTENCES BECOME NARRATIVES, WHICH IS SOMETHING I DON'T WANT, I LIKE THAT FINE LINE BETWEEN PROSE AND POETRY AND PRAYER THAT DOUG DOES.

the job, it seems to me, is to build a doug rice in Spanish. you need to know beforehand at least some of what that should include. [no matter how you go

about it, you must realize that you are doing the
work, you must be satisfied with the spanish doug
rice, and that that is all you can do. you lend your
voice [and are lucky enough to have contact with the
writer, and all you can get from that]. i think i am
repeating myself, but i will say this: getting a
list of the music that he listened to when he was
working on this book may be the most important thing
you can do

I ASKED WHAT HE WAS LISTENING TO, AND THEN I
FOUND OUT THAT THE RHYTHMS OF THAT MUSIC
DOES NOT COINCIDE WITH THE RHYTHMS OF THE
MUSIC I LISTEN TO WHILE TRANSLATING HIM.

[and listening to the music],
to understand the rhythms. from what you've said in your email,
sounds like you do have some understanding of doug's writing.
"joy of repetition"—it is and is not repetition, of course

SO TRUE.

and is very important. Perhaps "return"
would be more accurate

IT IS WHAT HAPPENS WHEN PRAYING. THE VOICE
BECOMES A DRONE THAT RETURNS TO THE ORIGI-
NAL PRONUNCIATION OF THE PHRASES,
RENEWWING IT CONSTANTLY BY BEING THE SAME.

i think of Philip glass's music. it sounds like repetition, but each
return is movement, in a spiral, if you like.

- 11 -

i have been rereading octavio paz's el arco y la
lira [the bow and the lyre]—actually, just rereading what i marked
on previous readings, and I find that i had marked many places
where paz's description of the poet [all poets] fits rice. For example, "Although he receives communion at the social altar and
shares with complete good faith the beliefs of his time, the poet
is a being apart, he is heterodox by congenital fatality: he always
says
something else [italics], even when he says the same
things that the other men in his community say."
this says so much about rice, who is so catholic,
but heretical.

"transpose his rhythmic style"—you know, this is
borges' gripe against spanish, that it took too many
words to say what could be said in english. i think
there may be a number of ways to attack this
problem. one of doug's patterns is to break down a
sentence with periods [that is, what would be a
sentence if you put them together, has been made
into a "stuttering," tripping, whatever the right
word is. being careful not to overuse this idea, you
might be able to break what seems too long into
fragments that make sense

I'VE TRIED TO DO THAT, BUT THEN I GOT
"REPRIMENDED" BY AN EDITOR AND TRANSLATOR,
MY BROTHER IN LAW, A POET, WHO SAID THAT IT IS
NOT CORRECT TO DO IT THAT WYA IN SPANISH.
MAYBE IT WAS WRONG THE WAY I BEGAN TO USE IT,
THEN I THINK I SHOULD WORK ON THAT ALSO. .

[here is where the idea of cutting adjectives might help, too].

"if doug has any sources..."—of course he does. and
i think this might be quicksand for you. trying to
comprehend this seems beyond the possible [think of
borges' pierre menard here

NEVER THOUGHT OF THAT, BUT YEAH. . .].

more than likely, this would be a distraction [although he does
have a collection of classical sentences that he uses. For example,
at top of page 158 of skin prayer ms,
"Today, my mother comes and goes...", which is
eliot, of course. this is a phrase that recurs
throughout doug's writing.] but most of the time,
his source material is so "layered," as he calls it,
or buried, that only an obsessive graduate student
could find what source he is using. there are also
book titles, phrases, lines of songs, etc, used
straight. i think his best writing comes when he
escapes the "pirating" method and comes up with
brilliant sentences only he could write. [a side
note: when i was reading skin prayer, i wrote on p.
60 "anais nin," not meaning it in a good way, only
to learn that doug had, since writing what i read,
gone to nin and pirated some words and put them in
that same place. that is, i read nin to be there
before he put her words in].

i'm going to have to cut this off for now [i have a
time-limit on this computer]. will try to pick this
up on saturday. if you read this over, try to feed
me your questions/comments from what i have said so
far. i'll talk about burroughs, litany, and cunt

next time.

Adios

THANK YOU VERY MUCH, DON. IN THE FUTURE, I
WOULD ALSO LIKE TO DISCUSS HOW THE PARTS OF
THE BODY
THAT RECUR FROM TIME TO TIME IN HIS WRITING
(RIBS,
FIST, THIGH, KNEES) SOMETIMES SOUND TOO cut
and dried
IN SPANISH. I DON'T KNOW IF IT'S TOO MUCH SUB-
JECTIVITY
ON MY PART OR WHAT

PART TWO

ALEJANDRO: Don, I'M GOING TO DO IT THE SAME
WAY AS BEFORE,
ANSWERING OR SPEAKING ALONGSIDE YOUR OWN
WORDS:

DON HARROLD: about the 'cut up'—as far as i can tell [doug
is
not forthcoming about specifics of method], doug
collects phrases, sentences, etc, for use

Alejandro: IT'S SORT OF MIND SCAVENGING. . . WHEN
I WAS YOUNG, ABOUT
SEVENTEEN, I STARTED TO WRITE POETRY, THEN
FICTION;

THE WAY I WORKED WAS THAT I STARTED LISTEN-
ING TO THE
MUSIC (U2'S THE JOSHUA TREE BEING A BIG FAVOR-
ITE) AND
FOLLOWED THE SOUNDS OF THE WORDS. . . I UN-
DERSTOOD THE
LYRICS, I JUST WASN'T INTENTLY LISTENING TO
THEIR
CONTENT, MORE TO THE WAY THEY SOUNDED,
AND I
TRANSLATED THAT SOUND INTO SPANISH, THE
NARRATIVE FLOW
WAS BEING LED BY THIS EXERCISE, SO, FOR EX-
AMPLE, IF I
HEARD A MORRISEY SONG CALLED Bengali in platforms,
AND
HE SAYS THOSE WORDS IN THE SONG, I SOMEHOW
TRANSPOSED
THAT SOUND AND TURNED IT INTO Benjamin y sus
zapatos
de plataforma, I STILL DON'T UNDERSTAND THE
CONNECTIONS, JUST THE FACT THAT I WAS ENAM-
ORED WITH
THAT SIMPLE METHOD, MUCH MORE REFINED IN
DOUG'S,
BECAUSE HE TENDS TO CATCH HIMSELF WITH THE
PHRASE, OR
THE LINE, AND HE THEN JUST SINKS IT INTO THE
LINES OF
THE TEXT.

BY THE WAY, I WAS HEAVILY REPRIMENDED BY THAT
METHOD,

SOMEONE TOLD ME THAT MY FIRST WORK WAS VERY
HYPOTHALAMIC. . . I'LL NEVER FORGET IT, BECAUSE IT'S
THE SAME PERSON WHO NOW GIVES ME THE WORST ADVICE WHEN
IT COMES TO LITERATURE, AND HE WAS SUPPOSED TO BE MY
MENTOR. WELL, SORRY FOR THE PERSONAL EXPE-RIENCE
INTERVENTION HERE.

DON: probably also simply goes to specific sources for
> stuff he knows is there, as he works—that is, when
> he reaches a spot where he wants deleuze, he goes to
> one of deleuze's books. in mugwump [sic?], he leans
on faulkner [sound and fury and absalom, absalom]

Alejandro: ITHOUGHT SO

DON: a lot, but many others in there, too. of course, the
first piece in skin prayer, on acker, uses many
> things from acker's writings [the tone in this piece
> is elegiac]. litany of our body, the last piece in the first section, is
> very personal, using the words of the women
> involved, and bringing to bear words from other
> sources [the descriptive word for that piece, for
me, is "staccato"]

ALEJANDRO: THIS IS VERY USEFUL, BECAUSE
LITANY HAS BEEN ONE OF THE MOST DIFFICULT

PIECES, AND
THAT TONALITY, AT LEAST I THINKS, IS NOT TOO
COMMON IN
MEXICAN SPANISH.

DON: for me, those two pieces are the
> reason for the book, and are at the same time
> unbearably long, because of their intensity. doug is
> still playing with litany, although he is supposed
> to turn the manuscript in a day or two [litany will
> probably be broken up with spaces between segments].
>
> the poetics of reverie [title] is from gaston
> bachelard. don't know if much of the wording is
bachelard's.

ALEJANDRO: DON'T THINK SO, BACHELARD'S
DESCRIPTIONS, TO ME, ARE MADE OF AIR, DOUG'S
ACTIONS
RITES AN PASSAGES ARE MORE SUFFOCATING,VERY
CONSCIOUS
OF THIS

DON: of course, catholic litanies and
> various rituals are used—some specific wording—in
> various pieces, not only the litany one—teresa is
> st. teresa, as you probably know. the catholic angle
> is probably the most important source you could go
> to for the first part. the pittsburgh set
> [anti-oedipus] is a whole different rhythm
> [actually, earlier writing]—something like urban
pastoral [to be neruda about it]

ALEJANDRO: AT FIRST, I WAS
OVERWHELMED BY SOME PARTS OF THIS, BECAUSE
IT IS QUITE
A DIFFERENT FORM.

DON: the point about
> rice and his sources is this: he is a synthesizer as
> much as a pirate or any other word he uses for what
> he does. he can pull together, in his head, his vast
> array of reading—as any good reader can—but does
> so in a utilitarian way, able to find specific words
> for his purposes [there is chance involved, too, you
understand].

ALEJANDRO: THIS IS PART OF WHAT I WAS TELLING
YOU
ABOUT, THE PROCESS I USED A LONG TIME AGO
>

DON: better get on the discourse on "cunt."
> you do not want to use traditional words like
> "vagina"—traditional in the medical anatomy sense.
> what you are after is to make "street anatomy"
> poetic. is there a word that mexican women use here?
> "cunt" seems to be the word preferred by american
> women. from middle english "cunte", but the more
> useful source for me is the latin "cunnus"
> [vulva]—is there a spanish word derived from the
> same source? you do not want the equivalent to
> "pussy," you understand, because that word has too
> many associations [cats, etc], where "cunt" has no
> such connections.

>
> i guess from your standpoint, you need to go for the
> "dirty" word, but your job is to make it more than
> dirty. to "elevate" it is not the right
> idea—possibly just to make it poetic is
> correct—you use such words to erase distance to the
> body, as medical terms do—to be sensual without
> being obscene—if you understand the difference
> between obscene and pornographic—doug and i have
> debated that for years. ok to be porn, but not
> obscene [clinton is porn, bush is obscene, if you
get that].

ALEJANANRO: YOU KNOW WHAT I JUST REALIZED, AND WHY IT
IS SO DIFFICULT TO COME UP WITH A GOOD CHOICE FOR
CUNT: BELIEVE ME, THERE IS NO SUCH THING AS A POETIC
REFERENCE FOR CUNT IN SPANISH, IT IS EITHER TOO
TECHNICAL OR SEXIST AND DEMEANING. . .HEY JUST ANALYZE
A LITTLE BIT OF OUR HISTORY AND YOU'LL UNDER-STAND WHY.

I STILL HAVE TO WORK ON THAT MATTER.
>
DON: got to cut this off again. shall await
> response—what do i need to expand on? clarify?
> where do we need to go from here?
>

> ah, an addition: it might help you to send some
> specific examples where you are having
> problems—doug's sentences, along with some
> tentative translations [i can deal with spanish on
> the page, with english beside it], and we could see if that helps
you figure some things out.

ALEJANDRO: I'LL SEND
YOU A COPY OF Because the night, IN SPANISH, SO YOU
CAN SORT OF START FROM THERE IF YOU LIKE.
AGAIN, THANK
YOU VERY MUCH FOR YOUR HELP.
>
> harrold
> KURTZ.

Unquiet Souls

In loving memory of Kathy Acker, whose gentle heart and kindness stays with me.

I seek the nerves under your skin.
—Patti Smith

Preface To Unquiet Souls

Doug Rice is haunted—by what, we can only guess. He is trapped; he goes nowhere. He is a modern-day hysteric, a psychoanalyst's dream. He writes the same thing over and over, runs the same spinning track, as if somehow, through the repetition of extremes, he could eliminate the trauma, break its foul-smelling, icy-fingered spell. Only it is a spell of beauty – the beauty that comes from devastation, from the constant struggle to rise again in that roaring fire's shouldered wake. You will find no plot or answers here, only unbearable loss. The unbearable loss created by abandonment and grief. Make no mistake: Doug Rice kills us again and again and he does not want us to survive it, for he has been burned at the stake and is burning still. He is a ghost who can do nothing but plead with his bones and remind us of the choking beauty that ghosts bring. Despite his pleas, you will not like him. You will not like him, and yet . . . *Skin Prayer* is the power of redemption in the word when life has failed us. It has no inside or outside, it is only itself. It is the self-enclosed, hermetic world of obsessive need, a space where one can't breathe. And yet it is breath. In its own suffocated space, if we survive it, or are patient enough not to throw it aside, it gives us insufferable hope.

—Leslie Heywood, author of *Pretty Good for a Girl*

Malibu

Skin Prayer

(The sections in this story that are inside text blocks are from Lucinda Ebersole's *Malaga*.)

She wrote to me from Tahiti. Found her way to me with ink and skin. The presence of her fingers always near my flesh. This sweet, scribble girl in a white dress. She desires blackberry stains and lives inside the need for a return to the ocean. Her becoming a desire in language written on her body. Letters and bones.

(These words, episodic and guilty, at times false and uncertain, or unlikely as a photograph taken in a moment of haste, are shredded remains of a lost desire collected and then discarded by Doug Rice [a voice imitator]. A girl found these words on her skin and began translating. Writing. Coming. Her tongue. She stepped out of the shower, but tripped. Her body clumsy with desire. The clawfoot bathtub too deep. Our laughter in the morning wet with memories. We waited for rain. Longed for bold clouds and sounds of thunder. I become a living border changed by contact with her body. Her hand on my naked shoulder takes me to this place. Here. A body in desire. Her body waits. "The story I wanted," I tell her. To place these words from this mouth born in the desert close to her skin. Beneath denim. To write on the inside of her clothes. I have written for you. And someday the rains come.)

My friendship with Kathy Acker was most often little more than a string of long nights on the telephone. Miles and miles of roads and wires. Telephone wires that can only carry literal messages. We are left alone in our skin. Longing. The subterranean cries of desperation buried in the static. A gentle cure for suffocation. Writing each other in and out of our bodies. Kathy and I became lost to space and time.

"Come to San Francisco, Doug." Her voice trails off. "Teach at the art institute with me. Here you can be free. You can begin to think again." She wanted, she told me, to place her hands around my throat to experience the pressure of my speech. I still feel her presence around my neck, my collarbone. To this day I wear this pressure. Her. Here. Near my neck. This ring on my finger. The rope she made.

Late in her life, Kathy wanted nothing more than to cut her body into pieces. Small pieces that would stop the dying, the dying that ravished her body. An ancient, festering wound of incompleteness that threatened to replace the violence of sacrifice in her body with the ritual of purification. To seek. To lose. "If I remove my breast, this will go away. This will flee." But in Tijuana death is more resilient. All through her life, Kathy had written endlessly about dying but did not die. Now on the inside of dying, Orpheus descends. The herbs fail.

Through her death, I forfeit where I am becoming. Devise territories of longing that slip into water. Kathy's jaw in the morning. Her calf muscles. *Save your tears for the rain, she whispers, her body becoming distant. Away from my touch.* We lived each day in the kind of oblivion that can only create identity, that can only break and turn into a song. A tiny song that moves in the breeze, that cuts through berry patches. Blue stains on our shirts that want to cry but can find no tears. Just a tearing into a silent body. Write from the inside out. Do not hesitate until the flower bleeds. The anxiety of the orchard. The scent of eucalyptus near her thigh. Jasmine behind her ear. In a forgotten time, from afar, Kathy touches my lips. The blisters of her smell. A music in letters that opens my legs to her breathing. For her breath that haunts my skin. I open my voice. Loose and abandoned words that want to be somewhere.

They will make you impure. Our personal histories written on filthy rags that are barely legible and that exist without language. Keep your wounds alive to the ghost of my innocence. To come to your touch in the night without words.

Near midnight Kathy and I walk into the deserted city. We pick up what others have thrown away. We fill our pockets with discarded moments from the lives of thoughtless people. Paperclips, rubber bands, soiled paper. Dusty locks of hair. Our dance of fragments given over to the rhythms of debris. We find a perfect tomato sitting so still that we thought that the world had ended. We think of knocking on doors to find the owner of the perfect tomato. But then Kathy bites into it. Her gold tooth in red.

Without knowing. Somehow in our dreams we get away. We stand outside Barneys looking in the display window like children with all their wanting and their laughter. Her leather coat like some other skin that covers her, that warms her, that saves her. She tugs at my sleeve. "Look at the green of that blouse, Doug."

There's a lot, Kathy, that we do not see.

***

Kathy exiled herself.

***

In the frontiers of Kathy's body becoming, turning against the pull of water, I became trapped. Stripped to the base of my desire. To marry the violence of this torment. To extract the body. Is this your body? Struck silent in a cruel and vicious manner by a hand across my face. No body to speak. Do not speak with your body from inside there. I think I am a girl. She gets to be a girl. While I stand away from the world. Waiting. Where I am. Inside there before speech. What I believe. Wordless. My family. My mother always saying, "Don't tell anyone.

Don't. Anyone. Say anything. Ever." I didn't know what there was to not say. I remained quiet.

Can't we just dream?

Kathy taught me to dream. The map of dreaming. "To enter," Kathy says, "the water world of dreaming." Lost children inventing pain. Kathy's red book. The triangle patch of dark grass. Her cunt. Wanting for love. Her heart betrayed her. This wanting too deep that came down to the place of words. For her to seize my bones. Her fingers break string. My need for disease. To live with disease. To desire a prayer to make my body into a foreigner. I dream of a return to the damp concrete of unforgiving basements. My own walking through streets in Sacramento now makes me become a prey to this fever of memories. Come home little girl. To my hands. His smile. *I am not afraid of my mother, father.* Kathy writes. But she cannot stop the rush of blood through her body. Ripping into her throat. Her cheeks burn. He led her down this road. Her heart a traitor. But.

"I will forever be writing my thoughts without order," Kathy says, "I will write without respect for your need." She feared she would fall. She feared she would open her eyes and see her father one more time. Her mother pushing her away into another dark room. Locking her in dormitories for disobedient girls. "Learn to be quiet. Learn silence." Golden rules to live in the quiet without a body. Boarding school after boarding school that discipline the beauty of soft skins into broken memory. *I want my father to know my father.* (Kathy resisted grammar and did not know what she meant.) Her mother forgetting and forgetting until the act of forgetting became her only memory. On many occasions her mother had forgotten Kathy's name. Her mother with her knives and her pills. "Please take the pill that makes you funny, Mother. The one that lets you kiss me goodnight." Curled up tight. Not knowing how her mother's fits of rage, fits of humor, would write themselves onto her skin. To make them into sins of her past. Aimless threats. "I dream myself inside sex shows. There I am alone. Always telling myself who I am." Fathers stare at my body. Reach toward my naked skin. It's like traveling. Between.

In this world without end. I thought Kathy would live and live. From this day forth. Kathy will live forever. No beginnings. Only a world with Kathy. So I never thought to take a photograph of me with her. I did not want her presence. Those slight marks on some frail paper. She would be here. Present. Years later, Matias tells me that he, too, has no photos of Kathy. Just these marks.

From the first moment that I met Kathy, I had been made subject to contamination by the desires of her tongue. This urge to live through changed rhythms. Her gaze locked inside words that could never be spoken. This speech lost in dark corridors. Her twisted mouth becoming I. Gone astray in the spaces that separated her from coming to the saying of dry sterile thunder. Say not that word in the flesh. "I want to find a way in. I want to understand the brutality of being in love with some man that I have met in an orchard and whom I can only understand as a vague abstract body in that state of being where only sex matters." In Germany, Kathy drives her motorcycle into the trees. Fallen apples. Nearly slides off the road into the deep snow. Finds him standing there. A dark forest. Still. The smell of a river. *I am sorry this is not you, Doug.* To live without meaning. Beyond the comfort of words. Following into this desire. To. The image of a red rock with no water burning under her skin. Bone. *An uneasy song becoming noise.* Rude mouth music. Rough hearts caught on the inside of her throat.

Beneath the needle inside the pain of cancer, Kathy Acker invented someone to help her make her body.

***

I forced myself to do what I wanted to do.

***

"I am in my body now," she said. A recording, the echo of her voice, left on my answering machine. Oct. 2nd, 1997. Last words. But there can be no last words. Final rites for the living. Forgive me these dark and wild nights. This sin. A warehouse by The Kitchen. I can barely recall the needles, the lights, the bodies. And her sweat. Absent. Kathy lingered nearby the turmoil of speech. Words unspoken fell prey to her throat. Years later her words dropped from her mouth onto the concrete sidewalk of the Mission District. She struggled as if she were locked inside a trap. She needs to return to England. "Medicine, Doug."

"I don't want to be this monster any longer. To be a loner on the rim. To live in parking garages. I want to be able to live without swallowing one more thing." Her mouth wanted to become disobedient.

It took Kathy forever to hang up the phone. Don't leave me like this. Now without her voice here I wonder if she has escaped. She said she could see doors. All along Revolution Boulevard we stumbled in and out of consciousness.

***

In death, orgasms change.

***

I become unknown. Look into the desert. She fades away from the present into color. Her skin covered with chills. Her body, just by looking, comes to the thrill of desperation. Goosebumps on her arm. Her desires become red and she walks down some lonely path. Kathy enters a distance. Comes closer to her own difficulty. Leaves streets littered with remains from careless dreams. She tears away soft edges. The corners of her mouth. *Be with me tonight, Doug. Stay here with me.* I have lost this. At the crossroads. To return to origins through languages. To revive the space that has been made to disappear at the moment of blood.

Kathy gave me skin.

I go to the river, am drawn to the river, carry my body to the river, because it is the beginning without words. Run out of Etna, down to the Allegheny River. The calm water that deceives me. That disguises its desires. Caelia tells me stories of water and dolphins. These words in time in place allow her to become water. She rocks her body. The rhythm of her seeing the world, hearing the world with this return to breathing.

In a dream I saw a way to survive the breaking of this body into loss. So we stood barefoot near the edge. Near some edge along a river. In mud. No one saw us. Or, if anyone saw us, we no longer cared about their seeing. Only our bodies in this space here. Water moves over our bodies. To become awake on the inside of skin. Her body alert to this becoming. Brings us to a present. To live with water washing our skin. I want to come to your body with my body. To come near your skin. To wound. To seize. I take hold of your bones. You close your mouth. Somehow you keep your eyes open and you see something blue. She once told me that I could make her come to blood just by touching her skin. That with each touch she began bleeding.

This forgery of forgetting.

Kathy taught me the disease of writing. The foreign spaces that open to discipline. The uncontrollable pain of another's fingers penetrating the line of desire. "Saint Birgittia of Sweden," Kathy told me while we were standing in some basement outside of Buffalo, "declared that any Pope who permitted priests to marry should have his eyes plucked out, his tongues, his lips, nose, ears, hands, and feet hacked away, and all the blood drained out of his body until his cold corpse was thrown to wild beasts to devour."

Spiritually speaking of course.

Our lips came. Close to our tongues. To find our way to

longing.

—You detour everything I say.

—When is a boy not a boy?

We use indirect tongues that we have brought back with us from the desert. We suffer inside uncomfortable moments of this infection. She breaks one of her scabs open. Crooked nails, chipped, she irritates these layers of her skin until there is blood. I can do this with my own body.

"Do you like walls, Doug?"

"I need to be on the inside, Kathy. This need to be near the matter. Your making of the fluids of your body."

Before Kathy had her first tattoo written onto her skin, she spoke. "I have been afflicted by some highly disturbing symptoms caused by the mere act of writing." To see that which is before our eyes. To lift the veil and speak. I speak but do not speak. I leave to seek the emptiness that darkens my veins.

I know how to make a reader come.

To follow me.

I can heal readers of their desires. I can make readers exit themselves. "But the primary pleasure is not for the reader," Kathy says. "It is for me."

Helene calls me and says, "I feel like I am protecting myself from reading you. I keep some layer of skin over this space that wants to open. That hungers. So, I read you safely from over here. I am frightened by your inside, Doug. I know to stay away from this." Out of the corner of my eye, I search for deserts. "I hold back from reading you."

Kathy took me by her hand. Led me into an awkward land to live among lost souls. And we walked down the empty streets, cold, in Providence. To find the ocean. To step into movement. *I am bleeding tonight.* My body is unable to reject her way for speaking. The words she says wait on the floor. Like her words, she wants to serve. To survive. "I know this desire," Kathy says, "to be owned. To be placed." There is an antagonism between my body and my language. I am separated. Someone had broken into her body in an ungodly manner. Kathy became distressed by this slash. The fold. A thousand and one ways for saying. The new moon slices the dark sky. *I can see the fold.* The gaping wound. Flooded by rituals. She comes and goes. Condemned to say nothing but the same word. Again and again. The breakdown in repetition. The sight unseen. Unknown. In the same motion. I becoming lost without following. Uncertain girls with fragile hands led me to this other place where bodies have been rejected, expelled. We were on the outside. Orphans interrupted by sudden memories. The shock of recognition beneath naked feet.

Lose your dream and your skin decays. Promise to push your fingers into sand. To build castles too close to the tides. She asks me to fell her skin. Touch. Longs to have my fingers near her skin. The ruin of the years that have passed over her skin. "I am too dry." Her small hand on her forehead. Old from the sun. "I don't have good skin." I reach toward her soft body. Lost in the night. Promise not to ever forget writing. To write this body into. Her words come from places that break. Places that surprise her and too often are caught in her throat. They stay there. Unsaid remains. *I can't stay.* The movement of her hand over the page. Our skin. Writing is not skin. *I can't.* She is heading south. San Diego then Tijuana. Going away. Distance. There at last my body will cure itself. Will write itself. No need for me to speak. I want my body to take over writing. "I will," she promises. But she promises in the same words. Words repeated to me. There is too much silence between each word. Not the divine silence of breathing, but the empty silence. Lost trust. Her saying. To write is to take one's leave. To go someplace. Writing contains an inside and outside within itself. Away from itself.

Her hands shake.

"Do not care for me," she says. "Do not love me." Compelled again and again by a confessor's fever, which forced her to lift a small corner of the veil of her language. But only a small, tight corner of it. Then she always became frightened when anyone listened too attentively. She began repeatedly erasing the making of herself, this denial. Luring. Her blurred passageways. She confused all of her own images with tactile memories that somehow could never be seen. And contradiction. Words that worked against the body. "Don't believe my words. Why did you take these words, my speaking, to heart? What were you thinking?" She feared that such giving would condemn her to silence. "I am too far inside. But you are the only one that I can speak to. The only who knows this. I am torn without you." Never to come home always. No protection in the night. Just the quiet rejection of a body lost to creation of false words. But what becomes of words that are merely letters? Words without hope. The point of belief that falters near the river's edge. To apologize for this absence.

***

With beautiful emotions one makes bad literature.

***

In those suicidal late nights before every holiday, between midnight and two a.m., Kathy always called me. She wanted a word from my body. For her body. To hear. *Tell me a story. I need sleep.* Her gentle voice in her delicate thirst. Obsessive voice cutting into the night. A fist, a cock, a spike. Kathy's skin becoming a lonely child for just a word. Strict wanting that never dies. No one knows this silence. The silences we have just entered with Kathy's death.

Tired.

She comes slowly. These nights appear longer than those nights that we had spent watching bodies becoming unrecognizable. Kathy wants. Still. For me to utter memories of other skins the way a photograph remains marked by movement. Once I tried to forget not the memory but the wanting. Mangled bits of old meaning that have lost touch with language. We stood in some alley near Alphabet City after a reading. We stood in the dark where we could not see each other. Back then, I could not yet smell myself. This body unable to control its own life. My eyes weak from a night of smoke and pained desires.

I want to take you inside. Where you become obscure.

Not wanting to look, I reached my hand toward the place where her body was not mine. Her body. This innocent shame of some pain inside me. Kathy said she wanted to wake in my skin. "We need," she said, "to stop kissing each other because language can no longer exist." Her teeth in my elbow. The unknown smile of a girl locked in her own childhood.

"This becomes too much for me to take. Even with all this distance, the miles in between, I am no longer sure any more where I end. This begins. When I am near you my body is trapped in becoming beyond control. To be pulled down into the water that suffocates. Touch me. Your fist into me." *I want to fall.* But all we have are words. These words here. This memory. The making of memories. Can we form memories with words, Doug? This saying of desire. Kathy almost could not finish her sentence.

We had exhausted our souls. The core of our becoming. Disappeared. We desired in each other what was impossible. Ever to give. Stuck away from each other. In worlds of difference. In dislocated places on opposite ends of the country. To journey from east to west. Come. To me. Each to each. Sand, mountains, trees. Desire.

Only the unbearable pleasure of lifting her skirt is close to the desert of this loss.

As this was once in the beginning before speaking, but we could not find our way, so we got lost among our travels. Along the dead western roads.

I thought she doesn't have a father. Tenses resist death.

Can there be a subject without listening?

Rooted in absolute disaster.

A need.

To crash and burn with hopeless cuts on a hardwood floor. All the stars in heaven that we could no longer see. We became desperate girls trapped in fire. At the stake. This fire that burns into my speech. To hide from the fire that does not set. A forgotten muted voice that sings as it is consumed. A voice without history. In this instance of song, her heart breaks. We had a need to run into water. I am never alone in this water. With her here.

One night I began living inside the work of fire. For hours, I took pill after pill. Red, orange, pure white, simple blue. Bright lights, big city. I lost count. As a child, I had always lost count. To this day, I continue losing count. Unable to count. Took pills to the point of departure. Felt my body beginning to travel. My body rising to the heavens. Ritual of Ascension. Took pills until finally I could no longer think. I could no longer complete a sentence. The synapses broke. I could feel them snap. My legs numb but wanting. To move. I found another pill on the floor. One I had never seen before. I watched my hand. Saw my hand move down to the floor. To swallow without water is against the word. Against the body. I get lost in this moment. It feels like yesterday or just the end of time. To see you in heaven.

If I saw you there Kathy. For you to take me back to the moment that we lost.

In the darkest corner of my room I see wings of desire. More flames. A psychoanalysis of fire. I begin choking on the dust. Fear in my hand. I breathe in the line on the mirror and feel my body boil. Her breath left behind on my mirror. On the furniture. Her breath in my mouth. I imagine I am tracing white lines down a highway. Follow the dreams cast out at the beginning of *Blood Simple*. I know where the phone is. If I can say these words aloud, I will save my body from this odd death. The quiet of dying. Kathy telling me suicide is a verb, not a noun. When it becomes a verb then there is danger. To speak aloud, to tell this longing for death to Don. To Leslie. To Laurie. To dial the phone. My fingers, though, are too thick.

I know where there is water.

Some haunted voice comes. To me. Through corridors. My body wants for the water. But before I can take my body there, my nose begins to bleed. Cut lines. Perfect white lines that would have amazed God with their symmetry. When lilacs last in the dooryard bloomed. Or something with flowers enters my blood. The sound of being alone inside four walls. These veins given to me by some lost angel. I want to go to the city of love. Take me to this. No names. I lift my toenail. Create a space between nail and skin. Place the needle with the care of a small child inside the space. Cut into my skin and release. The casual shock of recognition. I can see you. A blood vessel breaks in my eye. I see you. This place devoid of songs. Lightning comes. God did not divide the day into light and darkness. The day divides the night.

I see her purple fingers and her toes. I see her toes. Of all the things on this earth for me to see. Relentless. Tiny crushed feet. Pewter pins stuck in some corkboard. I pray for God to take this away. To take me away from this moment. The present.

It is near Christmas and her body is blue, but her lips are red and they tremble in the cold. She stumbles over the root of a tree or some uneven pavement. *For you, she says.* But there is only presence. And the synapse does not break apart. Does not fall to the ground. Does not fade away. I got these bones. We are traveling out of the blue, everybody loves this body, down thunder road. I could taste you even then. Now to leave. I want to see a flower or a tree. But I cannot lose her toes. I need to see a magnolia tree. Something falls from the sky. If I could turn on the television set, I could go away. Come live with me and be my love. For a moment I return to those dead college days. I remember Elena. Saying this to Elena like I was some dead poet. And her unsnapping her jeans. Her dropping her jeans to the dirt anyway. Her believing in poetry like it was something real. And me in some haze breaking through. Jimi's mad fingers making new maladies of the soul.

Everything blue eventually becomes red.

Broken pieces of yesterday's dreams. Mad visions from the 1970s rush back to me with a vengeance. I am 17 again and lining up my first shot. Speedballing. Tapping my fingers on the sidewalk to some song ripping my blood. Warm bottles of beer with the labels peeled off. Beers hotter than the day. Sweating humidity. Musty girls lie with us on the concrete streets looking into the dark city night. Perfect beads of sweat on their foreheads. Girls that want to dye my hair. They offer to do tricks with their tongues. They lift their tongues with sweet innocence. The perfect edge of their smiles. "Put the needle here, sweet boy." We are in a back alley off Fifth Avenue in Pittsburgh. A night of elbows and skinny knees. Shooting hoops with the boys. Jeep and The Doctor pull out Sweet Baby Jane. A velvet cloth and sharp needles. Have a little fun before we die. I bite into my wrist. Julianne at my feet. Lovesick girl with her mouth and teeth. I want to stay there with her again. The sugar of Julianne's mouth. All through her blood. We were young and beyond love. Just bodies in flight without a word. She told me she knew of a desert. A place of endless skin where the sun feels like sex on our bodies. A place where a grain of sand on the tip of your tongue is like a purple dot on a tiny square of paper. To disorder the world. Julianne presses her mouth against my mouth. And we climb the city trees.

"Come live with me in the water," she says. "Through the fence there is life in the water, Doug. Be careful with the stones, though. They are slippery." Bare feet and the need to speak. Her distant voice through turbulent water. Near her skin, I have become less familiar with myself than with the ocean. In her arms. A deserted beach in the middle of the desert. Arizona. I force my way into the water, liquid, yet resilient. Light and sharp my body hesitates before entering. A fertile terror. As in loving where resistance is often an act of pleading. To return to the dreams of oceans and her skin.

Cutting. Please, Sister Morphine, turn this nightmare into a dream.

I was dealing with a fake I.

The burn in my body took me to the place where there is no thinking. Language undone. She's come undone. I undone. This. This silence transformed by fire. She was never there. Not really there. Here. Still, I see only her toes and feel my body moving. I kick the covers down to the floor. Out of bed. My feet. This body. To go to water. It is three a.m. All the clowns have locked themselves in their beds. Gold dust women cracking their knuckles. Sacramento in late June. I feel the plaster too close to my skin. With desperate longing, I try to refuse my body. To force my body to no longer feel her memory.

It's not going to stop.

Kathy tells me to never give away her words to anyone, ever, Doug. This gift I speak to you. This, the words, Kathy and

I gave over to each other. This giving of word to word. Our body. To open. To this very day, representatives from Duke University continue to call me. Begging. Wanting Kathy's papers. As if Kathy sent me paper. "Words," I tell them. "She gave me words." And never once pulled back from this.

I feel each and every memory, each and every pill eating away at my flesh. The mad panic through my veins. Colors without names. I see the marks left behind by the rust of needles. They come back to life. To be ground into the earth. To dig into the earth with my fingers. To find a way to live in the earth.

I try to remember the difference between water and earth. When I was a child my mother taught me how to make mud pies. "Learn this," she says, "and you can become a god." The coming together of water and earth. Lidia and I stand on a beach before the tide. We wait for the ocean to touch the sand. The moment, this space, before becoming wet. But something else. Something about being pulled down. Something about feet falling. Bodies that vanish without remembering. But I remember her wet near the edge of the river. Pull her close to my body. Haunt her with this longing. A dream that won't come.

Caelia told me once that she had seen a small child jumping up and down in a river. "The river," this child told Caelia, "should not have a bottom." To move through water endlessly. Until there is no beginning. The placid deception of the river that drags you down under beneath its own desires. I want to begin again to feel something. Her elbow in my hand. I find myself opening the door. My heart caught by a demon and kissed. This deep longing to return. I become her lover without following rituals of desire. Some wild animal pulls me. I come into the impossibility of living through this night into another morning. She knows I have survived this danger.

I want her hand to rip right through me.
Without asking.

***

Kathy turned page after page locked inside her need to push and shove her body through books the way sailors travel the waters without maps. Bold thumbs. Coarse calluses. Broken bones and torn muscles. The dangers of reading without flinching. Without turning away. *I feared she would turn away. Become lost. Separate her self from this. Here.* We had died to each other. Captive bodies. Deteriorated. In this life, we had become nothing more than a chance encounter between flesh and page. "When you read my books," she tells me, "I become dirty."

Her fingers wet.

***

January 23, 1996

I can't bear it, Doug, … depression depression … I am retreating into a new book, want happy books cause it's so dreadful in the 'real' world … oh well …

take care of yourself darling,

K

Dear Kathy,

There are people who never even feel depressed and who have no idea what they are missing. The vestiges of childhood. Living needs a sting. Call me.

Love

doug

***

I write on you Kathy.

I had perverse desires. The tendency to fall into believing everything I read.

This body stands apart.

My words cut her words off at the pass. Spaces. The violence of the meaning of our hesitation. She said that she feared she would become a termite of her own body. That her bones would become dust in her mouth. *I need this love.* The words stuck to her skin. Covered her in their memories. Suspended in their own dread. Ferociously religious in our longing to return to the moment we open our eyes and come. To speech. Abandon the world and fall into breathing.

The landscape of depression is revealing.

I hear words from a window. Across the street. Houses too close for comfort. They look in my window. There is no privacy in Sacramento. Small-town madness that can't become a city. To listen to another's desires. Their songs. To live without choice.

Come on be alive again.
Don't lie down and die.

Her love, I hear this in the sky, will tear you apart because she gives it away. Without a thought. Reckless words tossed casually at bodies. Youthful innocence, or so she claims. Dead metaphors. Words that should remain locked away. Skin so thin, too raw to become anything more than yesterday's dream. A fascinating knife in her drawer. She stands outside a door, kissing and kissing, trying to make a simple performance into something that matters. That can become matter, but is always and only forever a sad metaphor. A fleeing signifier.

Kathy told me she was unable to read any more books.

> I held her in my arms the way Burt Lancaster held Deborah Kerr as the surf engulfed them in *From Here to Eternity*. I held her in my arms on the beach at Malaga as the sea murmured to us. I longed to tear out the title page. Longed to crumple it in my hands, hide this violation so no one would ever know what he had done to her.
>
> Each time I reached for the page I could see her hand holding the book.
>
> Feel the brush of her fingers as she pulled the pen.
>
> Feel the heart pounding in the ink that had run from her body onto the page.

That her past was not there. Could not be found in there. *It just wasn't there.*

A young woman lingers. Wanting. To travel down corridors with invisible doors. But she could not wait. She ran down some narrow hallway. Locked doors. A man is chasing her. But we never see this man. We can only know that this man wants to destroy her. I wait in this place where the sun never shines. Flowing white curtains. Spring rain and that breeze off the coast. The disturbed chaos of an Argento film.

I want the spaces to speak, Doug. I want to show you.
There.
I carve her face in pavement.
"Look, Doug, between these spaces."

I saw men dressed in scarlet robes. Red and red and more red. So much red so deep into their skins that they were nearly invisible in their own body. Men tearing apart tiny girls dressed in white. Girls we could not rescue. I sleep in this place. I wait.

I have written this on my body for you to remember.

Little by little I want my body to disappear. To beg the truth. The unbearable pressure of Kathy's flesh bears down on me. To covet her body with marks of ink. Years later I hear voices. Liberation from silence. The determination to survive.

Kathy used her fingers at the edge of what she remembered. A memory that had nothing to do with her skin. Only with words. She had been forced to believe in her faith in the past, of the past, as fluid as any word slipping between wet lips. To be rescued. Approaching pain gave Kathy a way of remembering her flesh. "Do this for me. I want you to see me. Look at me. I want the outside to be like my inside. This red." The inside of her mouth a red scar opened.

For five days she bleeds. I cut into my own skin to try to make bleeding. She bleeds without will. I cannot will myself into blood. Pray to God for a blood that never dies. Her blood is of the earth. My fingers move into her. She is the earth becoming flesh. This stream of her becoming. She changes, she says, with each drop of blood.

You don't mind the blood? My blood. There.

Her bleeding comes out of the blue. Down from the mountains. "My blood comes today, Doug. This secretion of skin and blood. To secrete from my bleeding, through my bleeding into blood. I can no longer enter speech." We tell secrets beneath the sheets. Our bodies share words. We can trust only the night. In blindness we listen to mad hallucinations. We never were the kind of girls to take home. *Touch me here.* She pulls my hand to her. To here. In this white room we rest with her bleeding. This hunger.

To speak of this secret is to say nothing.

I know how to pray. I begin coming. A word falls. She tells me to hold still. Wait until I feel my fingers becoming red. Until my fingers are only red. Here with her. I hold my fingers in place inside her. In places my fingers move. Her body. Cunt down onto my bent wrist. I want my hand further in her but she is too small or too tight. Or it is the angle. *I'm afraid. This may hurt. I'm afraid I will hurt you. I'll break your wrist.* "Relax your muscles and collapse onto my hand." Let go. Two fingers two knuckles deep and twisted inside her. She stays perfectly still. I keep my fingers silent inside the inside of her cunt. Now, a third finger two knuckles deep. A fourth. She refuses movement but her eyes are frantic. I can see the flow of blood in her eyes. There can be no words in this much bleeding. My fingers becoming red. Her blood down my arm. For two days. For three nights. To not give in to fatigue. Her blood remains on my fingers. I pray I become her blood. She could no longer locate her bleeding through names. There is no place in there, she once told me, for making letters. Just a pause in her speech. To see blood without saying. This morning I am nothing but my birth. But I can't cover myself in skin again.

***

One night in my sleep my father told me that when I awake from dreams my favorite stories would come true.

***

"I want," Caelia tells me, "to have a tattoo of a tattoo of Kathy cut into me. For the archaeology of her life to become my skin. Did the ink from Kathy's tattoos ever get into her blood? Her stream? The flow, the pull of her life? I want marks, Doug. The physical markings, these remains of our desires. If this be your will, to put your muscle into my muscle. To not let me breathe." She picked at the dirt on her hand. Skin. I cover her mouth with my hand and we become still. This comfort of darkness. The shadow of her desires. When she writes on her stomach, she slashes through being to begin to move to becoming.

"I wanted," I told her, "to travel with you, to travel blind."

By chance, I watch her eyes as she continues to journey from here to here. Never to go to there but only to move through there to here. Caelia is always in motion. The continual fixation of the visionary. Caelia watches a mirage take form. Birds being born without names. Desires without words. Flowers between our fingers. Her need for water draws her to this rhythm. Becoming. We are walking down a busy street in Sacramento at dusk. Her body dances with each step. I wander. We are leaving this place and becoming the music of chance. The trees are everywhere. Water falls onto the grass. The smell of damp soil through our bodies.

"I would have to find Kathy's tattoo artist. The one she dedicated *Empire of the Senseless* to. He would know."

To spit at the mirrors that control.

"I want to rename the myths. Speak them in new ways, Doug." Caelia is walking. She is telling me her stories from the water. From Placerville, the hills outside Sacramento. "To live through it." I had become forgetful and was uncertain of what she meant. Of what her voice could mean. Her mouth. The complicated fluidity of her mouth. This birthing of words becoming. Near the skin. To say. Or, I simply had not heard one of her words when a truck rushed past. "I want that trust," Caelia said. "To give my body over to the writing. My identity to the visions of the artist." Kathy had once told me of the incredible trust of permitting an artist to write into her skin. Her body becoming I. She attracted me into this thought that I had forgotten. With this memory I come to her from across the sand.

Writing besieged me, took me by surprise. I could not refuse. This refusal of my body to make words. Writing through following is a becoming revelation. To dress the body in revelation. To reveal this body of language through skin. Not an exhibitionism that calls attention to itself. That demands to be looked at. This is the writing that cannot be said through skin because the body is not subtle enough. This is the writing that can only be written. The body becoming an image of betrayal. The voice of Caelia's breath breaks through resistance.

If we could only discover boundaries. To trespass identifications, any desire that fixes one permanently in one mould. One place without hope for change. To wait. Songs that we could sing. *In her mouth, I found gifts. Small words only released slowly in the morning before the sun. But these words panic. Runaway.* To always face the present, to move into and through that language of here. We wanted in our deepest places to carry language beyond the sentence but we also wanted to stay. Here. I begin sentence after sentence that I am unable to complete. I imagine that she waits for the ends of these sentences. That she stands on some beach waiting. I want to make you a child again. We swam. We walked endlessly, tirelessly along a dirty beach. Washed our feet in the water as we danced.

She disappeared from here and passed into forgetfulness. I was no longer permitted to remember. "Doug, you can understand this love only by being betrayed by it." She is speaking slowly to me on the phone. Each word a space opening and closing. To fall into sleep with her voice.

Caelia kept words on the inside. Her body on the inside. Words of her own embodiment. She wore her words inside her flesh in the making of speech. She always needed to force her words to come. To experience her words through her body. Caelia wanted to bring the words forward that had been forgotten in her body. By her body. She wanted to write on the inside. To remain on the inside coming. Bruised muscles tired from the mountains and oceans.

"Yeah, someone wrote on me," Kathy says, "which is pretty incredible."

"Did you ever touch Kathy bleeding?" Caelia looks into some river. She wants to find a mirror. Red and living blood. I can't begin to speak from within this unknown. "Did Kathy ever write in her blood?" These are the reflections that survive. I still smell her torn hair. "The sun did this." On my skin. Fingernails that have been broken. "Bleeding can be a cure for our need." My knuckles infected. This intimate desire tears away at my nerves. She hands me a shirt stained with her menstrual blood. In the beginning. "Here the beginning can only be present," Caelia says. "So words cannot write the beginning. A beginning has no speech." Red and quivering. Bone-deep desires. "I'm a lucky girl." She sends words across the continent.

Caelia taught her wounds to become wet.

To trust this journey outside our sentence. To be the barbarian of my body. Not to play with words. All those pretty words on some string that breaks. But to find the languages that bear down into the skin.

My skin.

This deep and unrelenting pleasure to write in and around your text. Sugar lives there. Grace finds beauty and my legs weaken. The movement of your hands on this skin.

I want my body defined by pain and ink. "I know your writing in me like blood. I don't know why. This flame under my skin."

"To become devoured by this writing. Rather than eat, I desire to be eaten. I want to carry Kathy on me." Caelia kneels.

She touches wet stone. "My story in this life," Caelia says, wit out looking up to me, "the matter of this is what has been ciphered onto my body. The body. My body. I want the tattoo of Kathy's tattoo of a tattoo of Kathy to continue to talk, to narrate the incident responsible for its inscription."

I beg her to press her thumb into my bicep. Or her teeth. Her teeth into my skin. The remembrance of things passing. Pain condemned to the failure of memory. We take a slow look at our remains. Memories lie most in buried fears. Memory beneath the skin. Nothing was ever so gentle as the way that Caelia pushed me to forgetting. Sitting on the balcony with our feet in the air. Her provocative ankle. The bone that waits. Lost time and a wet Corona. A half-hour late for some reading. In the breath before the music ends, the desert sky turns cold. We try to stand up. Our bodies fall.

We hold in this present the memory of what orgasm forgets. *The forgeries of breathing.* Her mouth opens. Mine. Our mouths close. "To orgasm," Kathy says, "I do not want to have to fall prey to forgetting. I want this, the pressure of your body into my body, to come to remembering. I want to maintain a separation between past and future. The island of this. Of being here."

The palm of Caelia's hand waits. Her mouth, salt water. "Are we forgetting here, Doug?" For a moment that becomes invisible, I see my gaze trapped. Caravaggismo. Light projected harshly. Light concentrated on her jaw. A disappearance of contours. We plunged into the night of ink. I struggled to separate my eyes from what I saw. "I cannot free myself from the blue shock of your eyes." Have we forgotten? Caelia's eyes had come to know something about breath. The breathing of language in seeing. Her eyes left a memory that stirred the ruins of my past to life. A wild rebellion against my own sense of desires. *You have seen something others have not seen.* Something there in her eyes that I could not feel yet. In this body. Something she had seen but could not break open into words. Her mouth close to my eyes. This voice that matches these eyes. Her smooth skin flushed with sun and pleasure.

We dream like infidels. We dream of a book that is locked inside a movie. And we travel becoming for this moment nomadic. A time of oblivion and thunder bursts forth.

"That's what I mean by primitive," Kathy tells me. "You don't quite know where the world is." I want you to break that twig from the tree. I need you to hit me. Kathy cries, her voice cracking open, "Does this pain have any good? Does memory which is painful have any good?" We cannot forget. Our hands try to become forgetful.

"I am afraid, Kathy, that my tongue runs wild. Becomes delirious." My mouth bloodied in the darkness fighting against the reins. I bite down hard onto the metal of her desires to come to me. Unfulfilled words on her belly. Scattered. She felt me. I know you. Pain penetrates me drop by drop.

With Caelia.

I cross the street.

We follow. Walk along the edge of the sidewalk. Our toes near the places of the things that have been repressed. My tongue is broken. "I read somewhere that in South America women wear fireflies in their hair to feel the heat. But when fireflies fall asleep they stop shining. Would you rub these fireflies to keep them awake?" I watched the visible beauty of Caelia forgetting. All that you can't leave behind. "Forgetting," Caelia says, "is always already there before we forget. Forgetting can not just appear." Our wrists somehow touch. "Forgetting is present in each word."

You have not forgotten enough.

In the breath of this moment of walking, our dirty feet carry us from here to some other place. Unnamed movements of tongue. Caelia tells me a story about some dialect of the Chinese language. One that always places women outside of speech. I want my speech. Your skin. To put my face in the center of your chest and breathe your scent through my body. To smell the sweat of your day. She had been running. Had run to my door. I bring my mouth toward her skin. To breathe. "Don't," she says. My mouth on her sweat. There can be no understanding without sweat. Fluids wanting to leave the body. To escape. The water of this body. To live on the outside of language. Always forever in the passive. Caelia says, "You will now become only an object of your speech, Doug." She utters this and all these other words that break. If only I could speak with you one last time. It is raining. Odd for a summer evening in Sacramento. But she stays away. A wanting to know. This her desire my desire speechless. A longing to not know which way to turn. Walking down J Street. "How do you think your body would feel, Doug," Caelia asks. "How would your body behave if I denied you the active voice?"

***

I loved her so much that it could only turn to rage.

***

From this day forth. She locked me inside these walls of tormented devotion. I try to whisper from the inside out. An obsessive dread overtakes my body. One that makes hope impossible. Someday for her to ache like I ache. Her fingers press into my throat. Under my skin. I want. I wait. At first, I thought this was just the English major in her. The theorist. Then she, while smiling, broke my thumb. Remember. You promised me. A voice through windows.

***

"It's funny," Kathy writes to me, "you guys can have cunts but what you can't experience is the real shit of being a woman, sexism, etc. … So tell me, Doug, about being crushed? Explain why it turns you on…I'm so curious…Are you slipping into the delights of masochism?"

***

In the mirror Kathy is coming to the beginning of speaking. Before I know who I am. She was becoming. Before I. "You will learn this sentence of your body, Doug." I refused at first to touch her. Her word. When we fuck we become each other. This naming. A pattern of speech. "You remind me of a very gentle little girl I once watched picking flowers." Kathy then told me that my mother had stolen the body of a boy from one of the neighborhood children. That I was not a boy. And that if I knew what was good for me, I would sing like a schoolgirl whenever the men passed by the fence on their way home from the factories. If I sang properly I could speak with God. Impatient to speak with God, I let them whip and fuck me. Girls. They played games about my body. Tying and untying my body to trees.

***

Can there be any other knowing besides this remembering? This place I cannot understand. This place you leave. All I am. Your forgetting has been captured by memory.

A woman from my past, dead tired ice palaces of my body, shows me a photograph of an avenue in Paris. Wooden houses. Narrow streets of cobblestone. Church bells. I watch her drift into the warm breeze. I watch her fingers try to return to the moment of these photograph. Her eyes close more gently than anyone I have ever known. She looks up away from the photograph to me. Mesmerized when my eyes see this girl. But, I do not see this girl when I see this girl. To see without seeing. I cannot see. I refuse to enter into seeing and find ways to invent narratives of desires. To see once again the past and a moment in Los Angeles. When she looks, she cannot speak. Inappropriate impersonation. Careless. My clumsy tongue is tied with the pain to say her name. Used up. I swallowed what she had confessed. "I have never been so free," she says. Her voice. "So strong." I lose her words; they drift out away from my body. I lose her again and again among desires to hold her into the night. This silence that gets under your skin. My skin. She carries her words away from here.

Not this.

"Aren't you afraid," Caelia asks, "of you becoming Doug Rice?"

"As a historian, I can imitate myself, but as an artist I have to resurrect."

Something being torn out of my body. As out of the earth. The way my mother would yank weeds. Cut. Violent uprooting of this my past. These threads. Lively roots remain beneath the surface. Tangled waiting. This longing to bloom again. To come. To the present.

"I want to write a book that produces forgetting at a formal level. To invent a structure that works like the torturous camera movements *in Hiroshima, Mon Amour.* A book that destroys the possibility for remembering. To build images, to give readers language, while simultaneously making the readers feel that they have forgotten it. A book that shows you something, then takes it away. I want readers to experience how difficult, if not impossible, it is not to forget. Flaubert was ridiculous. To want to write a book about nothing. Writing such a book would be simple. I want to write amnesia. A book that induces amnesia. Jacob's Ladder with letters."

Ghosts that haunt. Prayers to saints who cannot listen. I have become a girl so sick that I fear I should have died. That I fear I am already dead in this leaving. She walks to her car. Waves.

***

Dear Doug,

"after I went 'to sleep', he left a message that I should visit him at his 'home.' Understand … nothing of this is 'real' anyway. I love what the word 'real' means in this world."

Love, Kathy

Dear Kathy,

Your last email had so many quotation marks I became frightened. I did not know. Schizo-phobic by their very place on the page, quotation marks in the past, have stained my writing, too. Bloody remains of wars over memory. My skin, an ongoing flickering of marking and erasure where each impression leaves a trace of itself at the moment of its vanishing: a wet teabag in the sink, an ear of corn forgotten. The mystic writing pad. What is real and what is Memorex? What is real in the word. Is this different from the real in the world? Hopeless schizophrenics and depressed people are always left outside of quotation marks. Nothing but acceptable camouflage. Depraved and solitary movement in the quaint confines of white rooms. The fear of infection. The promise of what she says. I miss the burn, Kathy. To live with hunger.

Love

doug

***

Kathy Acker's texts proper are themselves something wholly alien, something into which a man could not be initiated. *Her writing cunts my speaking becoming indecipherable anxiety.* It is this very anxiety—kinetic disturbances in syntactical logos—that makes Acker impractical (not impossible) to teach, to write over and about in the officially sanctioned, industrial way of those traditional Grand Inquisitors. *Becoming cunt* against this God-given flesh (bone wanting to become blood), I am *remains* at the broken place. Stutter. Debris. I plagiarize *becoming indelible.* Look at me. You, you with your footnotes and your fleeting understanding, your passing by of theoretical rigor, think (fear/desire) this "I" not unlanguaged Acker is a simple castrated fetish. You, with your highly marketable desire for momentary signatures, imagine that this ink spilled *confronting Acker* is not a mix of blood bone. *My deceitful tongue* accumulating the confused disease of older writings. I am *defacing foreign* cunt. Tonguelingual spasms. Muscled desires. I (this "I" is not that of my original voice but the pirated I of a corpse, a dead city radio broadcast recorded and left behind in a haunted hotel room in a desert in Arizona) eye the body. I *creating this continual* I *placing my conspiratorial eye in real danger.*

I enjoy the cerebral perversity. I love the language—it is my greatest perversion. Men don't want to watch their women read. If you think about it, there has been a conscience effort to educate women for only two hundred years. Two hundred years in a vast eternity. Knowledge is power. Reading is sex. Better left to the boys. You sit with your knees together. Be seen and not heard. Quiet now. Tend the children until. Until night falls and then fuck like a banshee. In the morning keep your knees together and never, never, write it down. She might just read it.

***

A virus is never bored.

***

After Kathy's death, prior to my own dying, in the past—the far-off and long-ago, I am told—the law accused me of degrading textuality with renegade viruses and of sabotaging the innocent, the protected, while in a state of retentive psychosis. I have no recollection of setting forth such a deliberate plague of confusing demons into the world against the word of corpriright. Do you believe? Believe in the word? The word that cannot be taken back? Others, however, have known me to play with scissors. Running with reckless abandon up and down aisle after aisle in libraries. Have cut my wrists and bled onto scattered books. My blood flowing into Kathy's red words. The ones that she had left stranded on the page. The ones that she claimed were not her skin, of her skin. They came from nowhere. Picked up by pirates on the sea. Words seduced from the lips of cannibals by virgins walking the plank. But I knew better. As if our bodies are not the machinery of such speech. I seize hold of the moment of danger before I penetrate her. She hesitates. Her body backs away. Cuts into me relentlessly. *Look at what I have done to your skin.* In the mirror her teethmarks deep in my flesh I gently touch these red marks with the tips of my fingers

At the moment that Kathy dies. I scratch. I scrawl. Letters. Seeking ladders. "This is one of your gists/gifts, Doug." Rob tells me. "To convey the bluster, the pre-stabilized groping of perception before it can be cooled by the conventions of ordinary language. The trick is harder than it looks." I do not choose. I need cut lips. The slave of me that wants a life in chains. "It involves," Rob says, "the lifting of viscous skin, the skin of tense/voice/conjugation."

If I repeat the same text, Kathy says, would it be the same text?

I want to change intentionality. This I, my body becoming spoken. Writing and writing over the original text to reimagine this body, until a new text appears, reappears other to its origins. Instead of as an origin or as a deferral. A word repeated becomes a new word.

I need to be invaded.

"You must be viral, Doug," Kathy said to me. "I have a hematoma on my skin from where you kissed me last night." She had cut into my skin with one of her piercings. And I had bled. But stopped.

So I fall down in a fit. I decide to be catatonic. I am unable to know anything. I have no human contacts. I'm not able to understand language.

They call me CRAZY. But I'm not inhuman. I still have a cock. I just don't believe there's any possibility of me communicating to someone in this world.

***

I feel, I feel, I feel I have no language,
any emotion for me is a prison

***

I want to detour Kathy through another sex. This genderfucking. My cock near her edges. To preserve and resurrect and become not here. A testament to Orpheus. To resurrect through uncertain breathing. A speaking to the other side of disaster.

(The nomadic sentence is only always distracted. In the beginning is forgery. Viral cuts. Empty mouth. Disobedient memory— *rubbing itself out and rewriting itself*— allows itself to be read only to slip away. If Acker in *deed* writes politically, why is it that so many critics only write *of* her politics. Who's home when she's not at home? As if Acker's language is not becoming. As if Acker's language is settled. An open mouth is pain. Discipline and punish is never a road to fame and fashion.)

Whenever Kathy sent me her manuscripts, she always included instructions on how to read:

1. Use wet fingers to turn the pages.
2. Make your body vulnerable to your soul.
3. Do not read without breathing.
4. Be careful with your skin.
5. Use a knife instead of a finger.
6. Careless slips of the tongue make me come.
7. Had I known, I never would have written.

A month before she dies, she calls. Near the end she says, "I cannot write anything, Doug, without doing great violence to myself." Her knuckles always reminded me of the soul of a cat, lost and alone in some alley. Rags and bones. Quixote in blood.

***

——"I am playing at coming."——

***

Kathy Acker wrote with a dildo shoved up her cunt. This is not a metaphor. (Remember this always: dildo is dildo, dildo is certainly never metaphor.) Do you need a footnote? Bodies of evidence. (Only followers of Descartes and innocent cultural critics of late postmodern logos can have faith in dildos as metaphors. Dildos also, of course, tend to confuse Lacanians. Except those who cunt their lips on mirrors. I will say nothing here of Baudrillard.)

***

"Doug, I hope hope hope you get good and not just fetisshistic [*sic*] (therefore narrow) stuff … (Everyone's always pinning their sexual desires onto my poor desiring-body oh well)." (email from Kathy Feb. 19, 1996)

***

"I can't decide if we should keep this as totally anonymous as it is at the moment…but the sex keeps getting hotter…very strange the whole thing…I can't decide what to do and it's a bad time for me, re the 'image' business, my image in the world as a writer is really in my face due to all the reviews, etc. I sort of like anonymity but on the other hand."

Kathy

***

(Old academics at the peephole smirking. Young poseurs [academic in far uglier ways than "real" academics] gleefully embracing the "idea!" of said dildo [some "actually" practicing "it!" (imitating Acker's spoken dildo) as a form of authentic communion with the language of the body even as they argue against the possibility of any origin] in such silly, lilting theoretical numbness that one can only wonder how they are able to do their laundry.)

***

trying to speak at the very moment when speaking becomes most difficult

***

At first, I know nothing of penetration. *Writing body writing. Subjecting body* to writing. *Forcing body* to speech. Now, punishing my body, breaking into my body, I plagiarize that which rejects languages. Bruised mouth. Purple seizures.

Reading is a sex act. Most people read in bed. Holding and caressing the book. Touching each page, watching every word. Ingesting words into the body. The word made flesh.
I want the other people to watch me.
I want them to see me reading.
I want them to watch me make the word flesh.
I want them to see my fingers slide between the pages.
I want them to see how the words react with my body.
I want them to see how my body reacts with the words.
I want to have sex in public.
I want them to watch this sex act.
I want them to watch me read.

I need to talk with Kathy one last time. It is winter in Ohio and I am becoming blind. She broke something on the inside of me when she left. They say this is the place in the body where language resides prior to speech. She carried many of these words, my language becoming desire, away with her, in a tiny purse. These primordial memories that cannot be said. Midsummer in Sacramento. An early fire season. This impossible burning into my skin. My sorrow reached like a cry trapped inside a hunger for rage. At nightfall, I become intoxicated with this horror. The loss of sexual innocence. The breaking of waves. A shadow of my desire to touch her here. This scent. Before night falls and before sleep comes, I weep because I can no longer imagine another way for speaking.

I wonder what her bones remember of me. If she feels this. Ever. Could feel. This. This the this that I gave. Over to her.

The Body Is An Evil Guest

I take the body and blood of Christ onto my tongue. Invite God to come inside me, to cure me. Call God down from up above. Deep into me. Call His broken lips to my skin. I open myself unprotected for the use of His muscles. My thighs cracked and mesmerized with this sight unseen. Fat hands of nearly dead priests, pudgy fingers, hold me to the floor. The tremble of His blind bones awakens my tongue in this mouth. That which survives but is never spoken. Unutterable. Kathy says she has never seen me more tender than at that moment when the priest places the host onto the tip of my tongue. Walking back to the pew, I close my eyes, nearly fall down onto the marble floor. I dream that I am the sweetest girl in the whole church and that Jesus would want me to follow His disappearing footprints into the desert. If only Jesus could say. His words these wounds. To be away from the world and with Christ. With His arthritic thumbs. Alone, close to His deformed hands. Suffering Jesus. His joints on fire. To give Him my dreams. Here is my will. Purple blood cold beneath fingernails. To quench His lonely thirst. My red hunger for His cracked lips. The beloved sand of His desires. Then one day He came before me. Stood. His feet on the wooden porch. And He carried my body to tears. Body without words. I cried into the wildness of penetrated palms. The cool water of lost rivers. Touched the smoothness of His belly with my lips. Sought punishment for origins unknown. God's love. The bottoms of my bare feet cold on the rotten wood. I showed Him the places where God had punished my sins. His teeth into my knuckles. I wanted for His blessing. Waited in the simple skin of the innocent word for His quiet abandon.

The elemental passion of desire is contagious. For one eats also parts of oneself (saliva, enzymes, acids that decompose the food) while eating other things.

A Sentimental Education

I count Teresa's bones in my memory. Recall the night she woke my throat with her hip. That sharp bone so close to her desires to make me into her girl. The mere thought that I am her chaste woman. Naked and coarse. I become her unforgiving baptism. She found the flesh of my body near her skin. Touched me with her unconscious fingers. The ones that forced God to tell lies. Teresa's skin there beneath the dogwood tree. I kiss her with all the tenderness that a tiny girl could muster. In the evening we recite prayers against the bitter landscapes, empty skies. Prayers in the dark for thunderstorms. Late into the night. Our laughter breaking hearts. Our fear. We must say goodbye. *Breathe on me, Teresa.* My tongue sore with missing her.

We need to lock our bodies in silence.

Offering our touch to each other only in the invisible cracks of God's forest. We break our wounds. Open bodies, a puddle of blood. Wet hair, no lightning. Teresa hungers for rain, needs rain or she stays too deep inside herself, too close to the death songs. "It never rains here. Never," she tells me.

Her family, in some long-gone-away past out in the suburbs, sitting stone-cold, without faces, around their metal kitchen table. Tapping their fingers. Bread crumbs fall onto the floor. I will follow, if only to find a way to follow. Years and years pass without anyone saying a word. Without anyone moving. Then, in 1971, her father pushed his chair back away from the table, stood up one last time, gone missing into a land without water. Gone to some great beyond. Walked down some path that led into the desert. Dipped his feet into the wine-dark sea. A dream disappearing before the sun rises. Or just driven down to the riverbank by lost years.

Teresa still chases those tiny desires of angels. Haunted

girl of bone. She prepares her blood for me. Uses crushed flowers pulled from her garden. She places my finger there. I had
nothing to do with it. Wet branches come into my dreams, leave
scars across the backs of my thighs. Trees we had, in other bodies, climbed as children. I carefully lick her palm. Speak with
the wet of her tongue on my tongue. God becoming the salt of
her precise cunt. The wound of His son. A precious girl never
allowed to cross streets. This tiny girl desiring nothing more
than a push. The need to weave her body into a song. *Stay with
me*, please. But such words get lost. *I will come home to you. I
wander only to come to this home. This. You.* Tissues of skin beneath filthy sheets. She hides from border patrols. Nuns stare
out the window. They watch Teresa as she steps directly into the
path of traffic.

"Do what you need, without me expecting it." Her voice
comes.

I pray. Salt burns into my tongue. Teresa orders me to
close my eyes. To lie in perfect silence. The silence of early morning snow in the mountains. Still. No. There must be some way.
Out of here. The desire to move. The emptiness of serving her
from this yearning. To survive my longing to enter. Her voice.
She put me, with her words, into the here. This place my body.
Memory after memory becoming present. As a young girl, my
body made priests die. Awakened the unquiet souls of ancestors. Teresa, in those days, refused to tie my wrists. I waited
until I felt the warm wax falling down from Teresa's candle onto
my eyelids. Sealed shut to the world. The word. Becoming ashes.
Teresa bites deep into herself against the soiled and tangled
muscles of her mouth.

Her hand, hard, between my skin and my jeans. Tight
fist. Curled fingers.

This is the naming.

To be brave. Cut glass. We jump on and off trains. We

place quarters on the rail and wait for the roaring train. We close our eyes and survive.

I wanted to cut my hands off. To stop this need to touch her shoulders. Her scent. The pure heat of the summer sun.

I always wanted to be a good girl, I tell her. For her. To be this girl for her and if she could just come home. Again.

Why didn't you tell me before?

I become all prayer. All offering. She spits into my half-parted lips.

Without words, I desire her elbow. We become surrounded by the possibility for innocent pain. My rib, her fingers breaking. This need for a pain that is nearly unknown. Invisible. But we have forgotten that we know how to move. Locked in this stillness sent to us from some strange god without a name just a tap of a vein, I come so close to touching Teresa that my skin nearly becomes her. Between her skin and mine, a burning dream possessed us. Her hand. Knuckles. The tight elastic of my skirt and this skin. She closes her eyes. A girl of fists. Too much inside me not to be aware and not to suffer but not enough to become my soul.

She said, "If, at 37, you have not fulfilled all the love that you carry in your heart, in your soul, for beauty, it is no longer worth it anymore. Do you understand?"

I kiss her tears that had fallen onto the earth. I gently place my hand near her cunt with the simple idea of wanting to burn like the martyrs and the saints did. The smell of wood burning into my skin. These flames that I want. We were suffering, had grown sick with bad memories of knives that we could no longer forget. Every road she travels in her small red car, she still carries with her, near her own scars, the knife that we had found in a wet ditch. Bent needles in the grass.

Rabid dogs circle our bodies. We are possessed by their hunger. White mouths. There must be two or three hundred dogs circling us. We become excited by their tongues but say nothing. We feel their heat, eat packet after packet of sugar. I fire up a match, burn the spoon. Boil the heat of absent gods. She inhales the invisible moment through a glass tube. System shock. Draws the gods down her throat into her lungs. Holds still. Teresa climbs Jacob's Ladder. She plays with her eyes wanting to scream. Desperate to make her fingers wet. Teresa teases her eye with the needle. Ritual excisions. Thirsty girl dying for a hit.

Why do you do that out there where anyone can see you?

I try to say I love you but there is only skin and a broken faith. We recite episode after episode of *Batman and Robin* to each other because it matters. Matters to us more than our love for each other.

Teresa bites her own tongue, her teeth into her tongue. Cut promises. She goes on biting for days. Until she comes. Her blood mixes with her hesitation before this moment. The moment inside the movement of her opening her lips. Teresa and I take photographs with an Instamatic camera aimed directly into the sun. I hear Teresa weep. Her knees cold and white. Seven seizures for the wet of her cunt. I need to smell her cunt. In my mouth. On my knuckles. This fist I move into her. Here with me. She had nothing to say. Refused to look the other way. We suffer burning tongues. Tremble. She comes into my dream and tells me to use menace. We travel over dead roads. Cross thresholds. I smell the remains of her breathing on the tips of my lonely fingers. Smell her beneath my nails mixed with the dried earth, the roots of flowers that bloom among her tears. Her crying.

She wanted to move with me beyond pain. Drift into the deserts. Leave all the rivers behind. Forget the mud of skin and water. The rain. She allowed me to run my finger over the tip of her fingernail. This need to suffer from an endless laceration. She cuts into me with her need.

In the fall of 2000, I write Teresa from Sacramento.

12 October

Dear Teresa,

This woman is inside me. The one you told me to fear. I feel you. Dirt and blood tongues. I tremble when I write her. Whore in the hallway, stranded on the floor. Sand in her pockets. Torn lottery tickets and a five-dollar bill. Incompetent heroin addict. Needle so dull it is round. And her. You not here. I in the mirror. As if the mirror can see. How can my own body be this empty? To split. I know you know this, Teresa. Have felt this. The need to be split.

It is fiction. We invent fiction, my love. Vivid continuous dreams to save us from the noise. To return the holy to our skin. Force the holiness of God back into our flesh. I want you to get God into me. And leave our bones out of it. Somewhere over there. Outside us all. Cold clit, idle tongue. Word spasms. Her word an orgasm splitting my mouth open. She wrote words I was to say. She speaks in these words that I once wrote when I was a sweet young girl. This room, in the morning, is sharp with mirrors. My mouth full of you. You will know what I mean if you say each word aloud in space. She wanted me to learn to travel away from time into space.

I want to tell you other things, too. Things the gods say I can't write to you and that have more to do with you.

love,

doug

Dear Doug,
I did not know if I was hurting you, or if I was loving you.

teresa.

20 October

Dear Teresa,
Come.
Unsigned

20 October
Dear Doug,
I've just looked at two photographs of torture. I must have stopped writing. To think of you. I sit in my bed. It is still hot here. An uncomfortable heat. My room gets too much of that late afternoon sun. I wanted to write your name. To learn how to write your name without moving. To write your name while sitting perfectly still. I want to write you in my own hand-writing. This page. This hand. This desire. Here in this bed with all your words. I sleep with your words, Doug. But you know that. Have known that. My life. Ecstatic images can be-tray you, love. Only fear can totally measure *what is there*. I miss you already. Wish you were here. Need you to be here. Can you continue to turn away from me, from this? To repress wild cries and searing pleasure?
Love
Teresa
Her blood is still red on my fingers. Beneath my nails.
I suffer her words. Her hand cuts into my flesh. I wear clothes she has worn. Sleep under the weight of her dirty soul.

My skin tastes what remains of her skin. Her scent bleeds my bones. Once, in 1997, I think, she refused to let me fuck her. Two years pass. She begins sending me postcards. On the back of these postcards, the most inane tourist postcards in all America, she writes in a barely legible script: "Fuck me." And day after day she sends them to me. A picture of some beach. *The water is fine. Wish you were here. Fuck me.* One a day everyday for an entire year. For weeks she sends me the exact same post card. Now, standing beside her in some deserted parking lot in California, she demands that I not move a muscle. It is October. We are outside of Los Angeles in some godforsaken parking lot. A yellow light burns the sky. She ties me to the sentimental stillness of her words. I close my eyes. "Look at me." Beside me I hear her breathing. This body. My bones. I beg her to tell me the truth. Her body shaking. Tremors of a tiny girl whose cunt aches with God's parasite. Close to her soft skin. The blood of her wrists. Her jewelry, old from some lost country that has no native tongue, has never been named, cuts into her.

I want her blood on my tongue.

21 October

Dear Doug,
I am writing an essay on you.
Love,
Teresa
I scratch her face with rocks.

28 October

Dear Teresa,
I haven't felt a thing.
Doug

28 October

Dear Doug,

Ravaged by the anxiety of your silence. I crawl to you. Bleeding, the way you love me. Stubborn girl you press your fingers into my ribs. Through me. Up inside me. Three. Four. I need your fist. My wet fingers all over your words. You want me. Knuckles at the edge of me opening. I beg you sweet girl to push. I call memory after memory of you into my skin. Your modesty frightens me. I wait. Burst into a fit of laughter. You are my renegade fuck. You write in different words still. The body wasted against interpretation. My body would like to get out of here. I carry ropes with me everywhere I go.

Love,
Teresa

29 October

Dear Teresa,

With each word, I still taste your saliva in my mouth.

Love,
doug

Teresa liked the weight of high places. The danger of no food. Her dedication to desire. She found ways to torture her body with longing. Pulled her body away from my body. This bed. She once told me that in place of her need for food, God had given to her a pinpoint of light so tiny inside her that she was filled with words she had never known before. Fire and the sea. A garden desire that God had forgotten.

29 October

Dear Doug,

I traveled today. Walked the streets of San Diego to the grocery store and bought baby oil and salt. No one suspects.

T

1 November

Dear Teresa,

I want to become again your virgin. Unvirgin girl walking on a bridge thinking she is a girl. Stepping in and out of my shadow. I tell you I am absolutely ready to serve you. Layers of broken glass beneath my knees. Will scrub my knees for you with hot stones found alongside deserted roads. Thirty-three stones, sharp, in my shoes. Days of Passion. I sleep in abandoned hotel rooms alongside highways no longer traveled. And I wait as if her voice can carry.

Your,

Doug

5 November

Dear Doug,

You are not allowed to do anything more than once for the first time. It just isn't possible to do one thing twice for the very first time. Remember the kitchen floor? Learn, my love, to think with pain. You cannot save yourself on paper like a drowning person clings to a rock in the slow Sacramento River.

Love

Teresa

I thought if I held myself back from skin, I could dream myself back to the water. My skin pushed under and away from her desire, from her seeing me with her eyes. Every morning she swims in the ocean. Those eyes, her eyes, the ones that want to touch me. To move my body away from your skin. Then I could become a virgin here for her. To wait. So I am beginning to wait.

On Monday, September 4, 4004 BC at 9 a.m. (I think I may have the wrong year), she first touched my mouth. One night she let me touch her hair. I am the one she allowed into her pain. Concrete floors and walls. Her nimble tongue breaking her body out of the state of siege. The words we need, she told me biting deep into any idea I had ever had of myself, these words have become extinct. Badly damaged by inappropriate and silly tongues. Before Kathy died she once interrupted herself. Once said in the middle of a conversation that people like us had run out of words. That Genet had used them up. Now we have become lost in the wilderness of our bodies. We stopped writing to each other. From that day forth we never again wrote on blank pages. Never a word of our own making. Instead, we tore pages out of Faulkner, Irigaray, personal ads, Goytisolo, bad porn magazines, and sent them to each other. Now, when Teresa and I send each other letters, we kiss the words, make the pages wet until all the words disappear.

Nothing But Words

For Terry

She talked and talked
until she was no longer there,
nothing but words.

The cupboards were empty,
deadbolts latched, the husband
gone away, his name
ash in her mouth.

She kept the black walls
apart with litanies,
wove words all day,
couldn't unravel them at night.
Columns of words propped
up the porch, filled the garage
where a car should have been.
Cat boxes were littered with paragraphs,
non sequiters cluttered the stairs.
You had to watch your step.
Like dangling participles,
paint curled from the siding.

At each crossroad
she added another story
to the pile.
It would take hours
to get to the bottom.

Words pulled flesh
from her bones.
There was less of her
with every sentence.
She was thin, difficult to see,
all plot, no character.

One day, she was gone.

(by Craig Paulenich)

Marks Of Identity

(for Juan Goytisolo)

She wears boots, jeans, and a sweatshirt. Even in the heat of summer, she wears too much clothing, and still shivers. Overdressed in flesh. She wears these clothes for days on end, days without end. Never once takes them off, not even for a heartbeat. After an infinity of days walking streets, bumping into abandoned buildings, falling down onto scarred concrete, she comes home. The knees of her jeans nearly destroyed. Filthy and torn. She gives me looks, terrible eyes and dull muscles, that unsettle me. My body waiting in the stillness of a corner.

"The day," she tells me, "when you learn to adorn yourself in silence you will then become my girl." Her tiny girl in lace. She reaches the skeleton of her hands toward my jaw. She did not need to speak of her desires; they went directly into the movement of her hands.

I wear her boots, her jeans, her sweatshirt until she says otherwise. Her body caresses me when I wear her clothes. Her scent becomes my skin. I move inside her becoming. The soil of her body. Her smell comes forth. Dirty clothes she has refused to clean. To wash away. Those places in her clothes where her body had worn the cloth smooth or through. These places of desire are like carrying a photograph of her with me. I no longer recognize myself in her clothes. Her tears. Her sweat. Becoming to her body. This near skin of my skin to hers. Days climbing in the mountains. My own small memory of being a girl. Invisible body, poetic and confessional. My need to interpret and remember. Unlike a photograph, clothes cannot remain innocent. Cannot refrain from the skin. I mourn the loss of this body of my childhood.

When her days of bleeding end, she becomes distraught. She wants to stay with her blood. Swim in the river with angel children. Walk across wooden floors in her bare feet. To bleed. Continue. Without stopping. She counts stars that appear to want to fall from the sky. This want. To be penetrated so severely that I stumble when I walk. On my knees. I rub my adolescent language against her blood. Years of lost intimacy reaching toward a long-forgotten object. She has awakened in the night, the middle of darkness becoming light, and has hidden signs that cannot be read beneath stones.

She raises her fingers to her lips, and smiles. I had once contemplated kissing myself in the mirror. Creepy and cute. The strange desires for coupled sameness. Can you say the difference? Just a little hole.

In ancient dreams my ankles grow swollen. My body becoming a dead tragedy nearly forgotten. Even on the shores of Greece. Days of brilliant clarity. Laws of fathers murdered by misbegotten daughters. The soles of my feet rubbed raw by sand. Meat blisters. Thirty-three days in alleys, random doorways, burnt-out old buildings. A stone cutting into my bones for each day. She has lived her life writing all kinds of broken words crooked onto the inside of her clothes. All over the house. On walls. Into mirrors. She scribbled random words in red ink. Words that had no matter. Absent desires. Unreal scripts. She wants to live inside the words that she claimed she had stolen from late night movies. Ecclesiastic spasms. Her body wrapped in the perfect narratives of her own device. This deceit of narrative form.

With rose petals I smooth her flesh.

I want you to understand.

I want you inside out.

To know her body. To be aware of her body on mine, in me. I stare into space because of you. The letter I never sent.

Locked in a red box turning into blue litter. A mix of disgrace and love. The shelter of your eyes.

You need to take me over.

She opened my heart. I began telling stories. Not the invented tales of mythical travel but the dirt of this body. Those stories. Pulled the ruins forward. Brought them to the trauma of my skin. A promise never kept. Petrified blood in words.

We go to yard sales. Buy whatever fragments of clothes that we can fit our bodies into. We talk to the people selling their clothes. Talk to their neighbors. Try to force them to confess. We want to know where they have worn these clothes. We want to know if they hung them on a clothesline to dry in the spring air. Later, we walk to recycled clothing stores. Try on nearly everything in the store. Then we leave the clothes behind. We watch others buy clothes we have donated to Goodwill. We follow them down streets. We wait. We keep an eye out for our clothing to appear on other bodies. We invent stories. Dreams.

We dress away from the present moment but we do so without nostalgia. Dressed in the dead years of old and worn-down clothes. Held together by the random sewing of delusional schizophrenics who stand in the rain and smile at the tickling nature of wet water falling from the sky.

I lick orange blood from her thigh. Her words. I can feel her words at the edge of my skin. Against my flesh her words irritate my desires and I nearly come to know the valley of her throat. But she pulls her mouth away from my lips. Looks into the distance for some river and offers me, against the word of God, the tight insides of her innocent thighs.

The Poetics Of Reverie

Humility cannot be sought; it can only be given in private.

Laure pulled me into a house where a family had once lived. "Smell the walls." She had forgotten the chains. But she knew how to smile and she knew how cold the nights could be in Pittsburgh. We stood in the center of this house with our lips uncertain of their own desires. "Have you ever felt," Laure asked me, "a pain that you enjoyed? One that you wanted to endure? One to live your life with? What have you seen only inside of that pain?"

Hardwood floors. Pavement in the alley. Splinters. The distress of a rash.

Don't touch yourself there. You will spread it. The disease will go where your hands go.

Laure clipped my fingernails too close to the skin. Blood forced me to keep my fingers in my mouth until the bleeding stopped. She always tried to stun my fingertips with fire. Flames. She lit matches, burned the very tips of my fingers with these flames. Sometimes she used candles. Held one finger at a time in the blue of the flame. I sweated and screamed. She called this heat the agony of God's joy. And she would know. After all she had been with God, eaten at His table, wiped gravy from His chin. The neighbors doing their laundry and listening to country and western music. Laure said, if I would just sit still, to learn stillness, she could burn my fingerprints off my fingers. Signatures of my flesh she called them. She'd burn them away, then I could commit crimes. Any crime without leaving behind traces. I could touch bodies and no one would ever know. Invisible thief, a haunting. She pressed her fingers close to her lips.

There is no writing of humility. Can be no writing of

humility. Writing is only writing. A pull into the Allegheny River off the Smithfield Street Bridge. Humility can only be forever foreign to desire. The writing of words onto the page, that desire for humility, is little more than a becoming of impossible. Simple scriptures imagined by refugee sinners before the act. Little boys and girls use words. Laure and I put our bodies there in the present away from the need for speech. Commandments in stone. A lightning bolt strikes the burning bush. Laws of the flesh. Laws against the desire of becoming. God breathing through the desires of men and women. Lost children roam the riverbanks. Words spoken in the earth prior to the act that distrusts the body. The language that disrobes the want to be loved. If you can imagine this in writing, if you can bring this to words, then humility disappears.

I long for her to tear open my skin in the presence of Christ. In a basement, she drove me out of my mind back into my body. Hand. Fingers. Thumb. She had nothing to say. Not a single word. Pounded me with the muscles of her cunt. My body collapsing on the muddy earth. She pushed my knees apart. Said something about sins.

Laure and I stood barefoot. "I need to know," Laure said. Branches at our feet. Rocks cut into our skin. "Someone bring me some water."

I tried to feel my cunt from memory again. Hopeless. Come to me. She said, "Think of my fingers." Round fingers unlike my thin, fragile fingers. Bold and blistered. She entered me. I. Her forehead, I know her forehead. Metal. Bring me to my knees. Stripped for her desires. She placed her cock, my cock, her, on the edge of lips. Mine. Hers becoming. Stuttered. Spaces opened as far as the eye could see. Scratched at my eyes with her twisted tongue. Chained and brilliant she fed on the mud from this cunt becoming.

Just a sentence. To bring pain down to my blood, not

on my body but past the body into this blood.

A just sentence. *The more I touch you the more I want.*

Laure longs to return to those days when she did not need to open her mouth. Without saying, Laure cuts her wrists. Without saying, I penetrate her cuts. A sanctuary for this cutting.

The body in pain stays a simple object. An inanimate thing. Blood lingers on the outside of our desire to speak. Laure's lips are barely open. To break bones. Walls written, scratched into, with the remains of our skin. The marks of our scars chiseled into red brick, gray concrete blocks. Carved into wood. She scrawled her scriptures, the faith of her body, into windows, mirrors without glass. She beat my forehead against the wall until I could no longer speak. Forced her name so deep into my body that I had forgot my own amnesia. A desire to be named. I became her name into me. After the tenth day, I had her name in me. Pulled her name into this body. Lived with her name cutting against the sense of my own understanding of the world.

Then Laure demanded that I begin the forgetting.

In the morning Laure tied me to a tree along the American River and left me there without a prayer. She deserted me in my flesh. Still, I kept her name in me. Day after day. Night into night. Cracked lips. Dry heat. Spiders that bite and crawl over my body. Then, after days of loss, she returned to the place of my body and began beating the memory of her name out of me. Took back all her words. She forced me to refuse her words. Many words were no longer part of my body.

She placed a raw egg between my knees.

The laughter of Medusa. Said not a word. Memory traces of long ago.

I sat still. Without words.

Do you sleep tight?

The prophet can only write of his desire. He fails to

travel. Words tossed toward indifferent skies. This writing from the mouths of sinners, from the mouths of saints can never become humility. Saint Teresa pled with her confessor to allow her to speak. To allow her tell the story of her sins. Of the benevolence of God. His willingness to forgive her for her many transgressions. St. Teresa tells me the truth when I walk the streets of Sacramento. Her scent becomes the forgiveness that she seeks.

To beg someone to open your skin with belts is to lie. To expect pain is to avoid the impossible suffering that makes pain possible.

I want to transform your body into a sacrament.

Eaten. Saint Sebastian remains silent. Unforgiven. He prays for Jesus to wound him. An arrow through his ribs. One droplet of blood. Not for the markings. Not for stigmata. But for Jesus to wound him on the inside. Saint Sebastian desired to be cut into by the saying of words. He wanted to be made to suffer for them. The refuse of words. This refusal.

For thirteen days Matthew bled without dying.

Because Saint Jerome walked into the desert to read we know nothing of his sex. A sly term that veils his beloved lacerations. The soles of his feet burn. The sand burns into his skin. The tips of his fingers blister each page. We know nothing of what he read nor of how he read.

If no one sees you can there be humility?

God brought us light. Divided the day into darkness and light. I see her become me.

There have always been too many words in the mouth of the Marquis de Sade. His bedroom flooded with sound and fury. Whores without cunts. Christ takes great joy in me when I am inside silence lusting for his actions. De Sade can know nothing of Christ. All those uttering women. Moaning aloud. Stuttering women with their scattered flesh.

I closed my ears to the melodies of Laure's deceiving

words. Still, I stand broken with her scent. The place of desire is the scent of bones in the sun. Skin. Those two nights we got lost in Ohio. Then her flight. Laure sits on a roof, staring east. Drinking martinis. Cutting her lips on the glass because we are no longer ever here. "The difference," she calls me, "I understand now. The difference between present and presence. I live in there but there is no here. In this movement." Her voice wanders. We stay silent on the telephone.

I seek the pain so great that no physical torture could ever drown it. A pain that will take me down inside myself to memory, so that when Jesus pulls out of me, I will release moans, unheard, so extreme that I forget my spiritual body. To let go of this.

Second Skin

By the beginning of 1981, blood had become dangerous, damaged by years of nervous desire. Disturbed deaths were being reported in the Tenderloin District. In New York City, sudden raptures overtook bodies. Poppers mixed in with desires for bleeding. Blood and glazed-over eyes in dark hallways. Everyone had the flu. It was the year of the piggyback flu. There was no escape. No breathing without coughing. Boy after boy murdered. The city had grown hopeless. Communal silence. There is no plague if we remain speechless. In theory, no one ever dies. As politicians kissed one baby then another baby. Kissed without fear. Kissed without protection. All these devils known only by their Christian names. Sweet smiles and soft waves. The speaking public. The people who die never existed. A just God's sweet and tender vengeance against His own flesh and blood. Clay of His image.

I had just driven back to Pittsburgh from Binghamton. Once back in the city, Janey found me sitting naked and crazy under the Birmingham Street Bridge. My body trembled at her touch. Before the skin of her bones. I wanted and waited. I could only wait. This waiting on street corners. This waiting beneath streetlamps. The glow of an angel. The loss of last night's twilight. A gleaming. A wink of an eye. Janey put her lips on my forehead. Sweet girl. Name of the father. My shaking hands nearly came to a stop. My feet tapping. Nervous energy. Dead anxiety. This disobedient body. I hungered for sugar, a slap and a pinch. My thumb and forefinger working on my stained skin. Pulling a vein to the surface. Breathing. I played with the algebra of need. "It's a walk into suicide," she told me. I was too bored to listen. We carefully did one equation over and over. Scary revisions that would have killed mathematicians. We did each equation until we were absolutely certain that we were correct. Until we had resolved our own doubts about the accuracy of numbers. Then we moved onto another one. Worked that equation with all the passion of Christ on the Cross. But we were becoming distracted. The numbers began multiplying on their own. Janey wanted my body to stay. To remain still. The slow shock of her fingers. The needle. We took our bodies to the floor. Rode the horse into the field. Another line of perfect rush on the invisible mirror. To see into the surge. Violet girls beneath my fingers.

I had become a testament to some illness.

Janey and I hunted down some rope and headed to the riverbanks of the Monongahela. Still, she made it clear to me: "No more blood fucking. Too much of a risk." All that squirming in mud. Mad fucks without a destination. *Are we going somewhere?* Night after night we passed needles over the campfire. Burned our fingers. Singed our flesh.

"Opened wounds need to be cured," Janey told me. "We need to wait for our skin to be healed." Janey kept her fist off in the distance.

What did you want?

To get back out and into my skin. This. Onto the street. The desire to walk along the riverbanks. To become wet.

Could we love again?

Janey barely moved her lips. It was as if she was not there.

Her tender cunt breath came across my eyes.

Janey's smile under the sun. Blue skies, no candy. The sound of a fallen memory. Unconditional love. We never violated our words. This trust, the breath we gave to each other. Words becoming bodies. When the morning comes, I want to be in love. Janey calls. Sitting on a roof somewhere in Oregon. Knotted ropes. The heels of our hands rub into each other. Blood sisters. I trusted her. She held her body without pity away from my body. In the over there, the place where there are no signs of bleeding. It seemed like miles of concrete separated our wanting to breathe into each other. Open your mouth. To give your skin over to me. My eyes could barely see her.

Doug.

In years past we had stuck sharp thorns into our flesh. Loosened pain from our bones. Not through idle talk, scripts, but through the desire to awaken new ways for breathing. We learned to burn our skins from our ancestors. In fascinating places we became our bodies. Raw meat beneath the full moon pulling at the tides. Janey wiped her mouth with the back of her hand. Her simple gestures pulled me to her. The way she twisted her bracelets, large red bangles that would be clumsy on anyone else's wrist. Dark antique buttons bought on the Southside of Pittsburgh. The fragrance of past lives. "You gave me this for my wrist," she said. "A bracelet I cannot tell anyone. From a sweet boy who lives too far from my skin. This bracelet cuts into my skin, Doug. You cut into my skin. I don't know what to do with this. How do you hide my bruises?" Simple gestures. One gesture after another. The way she switched her eyewear, changed from sunglasses to her regular glasses. A delicate touch of a young girl. She simply used her hands in fleeting ways that reminded me of a hummingbird near food. Once she took off an earring and smiled in the mirror. Smiled as if she had just transformed the whole world.

I want it now, Janey said.

Come. To here.

I was once a nice girl. But. That could change.

We are going some place where skin comes before bones. Where nothing can be recorded. I was no longer certain of our speaking.

Blood and feathers, we dance.

I refuse to come.

"There is no following," Janey says, "without becoming." We look down below. Sweet and wild fingers that stain our skin, that sound like crying.

She led me into a meadow.

You know she liked it.

I may become pure again.

There are other ways to touch origins.

In this new innocence, she had somehow grown terrified of her cunt.

Afraid to touch herself. Her body ached for the long-ago mythology of fingers.

Some nights she was too frightened to even swallow her own saliva.

Still. Her fingers remain. Stained.

I want you to give me over to your stain, Doug.

To make skin painfully new.

I felt my muscles becoming tense.

Past memories surface.

This dissolve of the present.

The stir of desire from the days of running the alleys. Doing service for the masses. Under the sheets, her body turned against herself. Janey made a colossal effort to refrain from her blood. From the telling of her blood. She slept like every other Cubist I have ever known: an elbow in my mouth, another elbow in my eye—elbows reproducing angles impossible for the common man to even imagine. An elbow entered my ear. Another ear, another elbow. And I came to realize the bold pain of each angle cracking my flesh and I feared that I would not be able to survive the night. Something new would have to be known. But I wanted this night and her in it. In me. Those delirious eyes. She never could see straight in front of her gaze. My body her eyes looking up, up and away at the moon. Another eye down below under the earth beneath the mud and she had this third eye, an eye of indeterminate sight. One that constantly sought an object but found only her own subject. And at one time, once upon a time, I could see her seeing me.

Press me down into the mattress, Doug. Don't let me move. My girl. Hold me down here. There. Break me. Into me. These bones. I am tired of these ribs. I cut her.

Janey's body became excited. Her eyes. She looked over at me. Across the space of words. Blood wounds. Those places where words can exist but bodies are denied. I felt her tearing me open with her body inviting me to come to her but then pulling away, retreating into her own body away from my touch. She wanted to be nothing but temptation. A tangled soul. This love. Sins of the father in her mouth. Domestic parasites destroying her from the inside of her words.

Words she could no longer. Swallow.

Could no longer.

To come to the inside. To be more beautiful in God's eyes. Faithful to her sight. To her looking.

Janey said to me, "We have to be more careful with the practice of undisciplined sex."

She feared we were becoming already dead except for sin. This is blood, not dust, in her palm. She looked. Her hand trembled with her need to find a mirror. A way for looking into her wanting.

Are my eyes still broken? Do they appear to not be there? To be traveling away from here?

Two days later I returned to our bunker, a house broken and abandoned. Janey sat naked on the floor, her back against what remained of the wall, hands flat on the worn carpet. She had gathered every single dangerous object from the bunker and piled each one into some decadent medieval funeral pyre in the middle of the room. Needles, used and unused. Knives, forks.

Small pieces of glass, tiny dancers we called them, lonely shards we had chipped off wine bottles. Memories of those years of shooting Maddog 20/20 straight into our veins then looking up from the floor as if we had something to see. A prayer book. Pages from her diary. Anything that threatened to carry desire. That might possibly create longing. A pyramid of flour. It reminded her, she said, too much of our island years with the angels. The dust on the very tip of our pinky fingers. Sucking each other's fingers. Burning acid. Wild horses. Angry. Tear us.

A way into the movement of a body trapped in paranoid motion. *How would you know? I mean know for sure that you are paranoid? I am thinking.*

Years ago she had come to have a theory. A need for greater objects. We could go to the viewings of our friends once they had died. Kneel at the casket and pray. Our friends that had the same addictions as us. The same joys. And we could scrape the leftover dust from between their fingernails and their skin. We would, then, live happily ever after. Jesus saves. All that glitters is gold. We began believing in fairytales. The kids are alright. No one thought to remind us of coroners or undertakers. The cleansing process that makes us cry.

"She wanted," Janey said speaking more and more often of herself in the third person, speaking away from herself, "to pull her teeth out of her mouth." To pull out her teeth so I would not seek the pleasure of her mouth. And then Janey said she wanted to burn her teeth. And travel. "I want to travel, Doug. I want to go back to the ocean. I need to swim there again." Every morning Janey swimming against the tides into the darkness of the ocean. "I want to stand one last time at that place where the water meets the sand. To be here with you there."

Outside this dream I dreamt in a cabin they stood waiting for me. Eyewitnesses of my derelict desires lost among ashes for Janey. My skin smelled of her fingers. She tastes of her spit.

Wet my mouth in my throat. I imagined I could feel her speaking to me. Words scrawled onto our tongues then released. Words pulled out of her bones. The first time we kissed. A narrow hallway in the Midwest. To come to healing. *This feels like dying, Doug.* Faked photographs covered the floor of our abandoned bedroom. Pictures that had nearly become invisible. Too much light. We had grown addicted to looking into these photographs. To seeing the visible traces of our memories in the photos. Our bodies crushed into each other. Our resurrection. The time we kissed in a closet of a friend's house in Borrego. Some party. A comet or meteor in the sky. The trick is to keep breathing. Fire up another. Temptation waits.

Perversions became apparent when we touch.

Janey loves cold bones, frenzied eyes, purveyors of the plague. I tore at Doug's tattered cunt. His cock. (This must be wrong. Needs to be clarified. "I"? Is this supposed to mean that Doug is working on his own flesh? Or has Janey captured the narrative point-of-view? Her third person becoming I.) Since I lost the rational use of my eyes, I slipped my nimble fingers inside Doug's tiny cunt. "Honest to God," she shouted, "he's a schemer. You see the stuff he wears? He's not a normal coffee drinker." Under Doug's tongue I became a motorcycle in heat. Experienced the inbreeding of pain. (This is not written in Doug Rice's hand. It has been found. Elsewhere. A street in Sacramento. While walking and gathering flesh. The "I", thus, cannot in good conscience be Doug. Not really anyway. We can only assume that Janey is responsible. She has done this to him. To her. Who is to say?)

Once we spit at mirrors. To see. How to climb inside.

Justified and seduced bodies in passion. In repetition. Emblems of torture emerge from the darkness. Her nightgown lost threads caught in splinters. In this room she gave me relics from the days she had spent in the rains of Seattle. Janey told me to learn to use my mouth as a form of menace for her pain. She had no kind words, no pretty words, only vulgar epistles. We searched among the roots of trees for the source of pain that would lead to salvation. Pain without blood.

These lessons that we live through can bring us home again.

In this dead silence we spoke of waste. We spoke again of the dry season. Everything yellow. Too much yellow. We spoke of the need for green. We dreamt of Shakespeare's green worlds. But Janey was gone, had been gone for years.

She waited to understand.

She wanted me to break her. Take her away from her life.

Still. No understanding.

How far can you remember?

Blood came today. Blood is rain. I sat in the corner with my mouth opened.

Janey puts her hand on the needle. The mirror burns.

There are no longer any rivers. A young girl turns away from turning. *I want to fuck your muscles, Janey says.* Real moving can't be stopped. Can't be planned.

My lips are becoming your lips.

Kathy once told Janey, "Love will turn on the lover and gnaw."

"Which one of us is the lover, Doug?"

I to you.

I have to get you out of my body.

You don't care who you fuck.

To get out of this body.

Janey watches for the small girl to turn. But she cannot turn. Desire drives the turning away.

Janey once claimed she had a memory that could save her from not having a family. But too much damage from the needle. She plays with me. Her father stepped into the ocean. His feet got wet. He swam out beyond water. Away from Janey's call. He swam as if there could only be swimming. As if swimming is living. His muscles cramp. His body disappears.

In the end. Janey. I watch her. Until. She goes down.

Kiss The Sky: The Rapture Of Hendrix And Saint Teresa

He said to himself: you shall not kill yourself, your suicide precedes you.
—Maurice Blanchot

Locked inside the raw muscles of Jimi's voice, Saint Teresa turned away from the desires of God and became once again the innocent body and blood of a lost girl. In a state of near-complete exhaustion, she traveled Jimi's veins. Blister-fucking. Just another shot away from burning into his bones. A mirror for his needs. Highway lines, yellow and white. The fairest of the fair. She was Jimi's misunderstood fairytale goddess of love and destroyed faith. All dressed in white, waiting, red on the inside. A kiss. He touched the corner of her mouth with the callous of his thumb. Pushed his thumb into her. Touched her so slowly, with such deliberation that she feared this touch of his would be the death of her or that her waiting for his touch would be the death that God had so often denied her. With each breath, Jimi turned Saint Teresa into an inarticulate virgin. She struggled against her own emptiness, the ache for words. Her body filled with frozen syllables that hurt beyond speech. Teresa's throat still. Her tired flesh in a cage longing for skin. For love. A late-night blister. Petrified words on the edge of her lips. The purple blood of barbed wire desires set free through tension. Her cryptic body shaking.

Jimi's rough knuckles brought her back to life. Away from the cliff. Home sweet home. Beneath his breathing, she reached up, birdlike, for the madness of his forehead. Her hands, small and pale, reaching forever reaching for Jimi's skin. Fingers trapped in the air. Dancing close to the light of thick veins. Hunger. Wet wounds near tears. He closed his tender eyes. Kept them closed each and every second they ever spent together. In hotel room after hotel room he forced himself to remain blind to her body. To look away from the impossible light that shone through her. A radiant light, too white to be of this world.

Her soul suffered his hesitation.

In his kindness, Jimi made first one promise then another and another. He promised Teresa, not in words but in the spirit of his body on her body, that he would take her to the desert with him. Take her away from the world of here and now, the world of God's refusal. His repeated denial. Jimi promised to break through the disaster of her bones. Destroy her desire for God and release her from her vow of silence. Words, the original sins of her mouth. Her ecclesiastic skin alive. Burning visions of pain and bliss. With his eyes sealed shut, Jimi placed his hand on her forehead as if he were granting Teresa his blessing. He lifted the burden of God from her flesh. His heavy tongue, thick in her mouth with wanting. She tasted Jimi's vacant words. Swallowed what she could of his desire. Mixed her fervent longing for death with his saliva. His teeth tore into her lips, ate away at the flesh of her mouth.

Jimi's fist entered her wounds. The mysteries of her ruins. Broke her body open to the light of God. Skin words. The blood of Christ on their lips crying for a pain so deep that they can forget their bodies and know only the violent desire for suffocation. To live inside a great, twisted confusion of tongues bitten beyond pleasure. Jimi and Saint Teresa, their bodies choked on the pitiful bones of stories caught in the silence of schizoid rapture. Distorted memories of pestilent needles carving into paralytic nights on the road.

No one left.

Just two cold bodies. The misery of the sun.

Teresa clawed at her anorexic body, a body of threads and thin tissue. Particles of diseased skin falling to the floor. Decayed bodies. It was the hour between dog and wolf, that hour when the world turns from color to silhouette. Teresa was such a pretty girl. In his arms, she went white. Laughed at the uncertainty of each move that Jimi made with his blistered fingers. Her eyes shocked by the strength of Jimi's knuckles. His strong hipbone. The relentless penetration of her tiny body. All the angels in heaven terrified of muscles. Looking down as if God would put an end to this. Psalms chanted in blood. Not the blood of God. She prayed for Jimi to give her his scars. To turn her body into his body. The body of some kind of animal. God. Her epileptic hands nearly out of control. Frantic for another touch of his skin.

Saint Teresa only appeared to Jimi in flashes. In moments of his need for severe discipline. Her voice hard inside Jimi's bones. Laughing at imaginary crimes, panicked mothers who lacked an imagination. Teresa pulled her voice through her throat, scratched at Jimi's eyes. The fever of her song burned, always burning, his blood as she moved over his body in some kind of disturbing ritual. The wet heat nearly unbearable. The air conditioner in the hotel room was broken. Spitting more heat into the thick, still air. Windows stuck shut. She cut into Jimi's fragile collarbone with her cracked teeth. Their blood spilling on the floor. They banged their teeth together, their bones, and spoke. Sweat. A world with no shadows. Red rocks burned by the desert sun.

All the while, Teresa's relentless tongue, lips, pounded Jimi's forehead. It was as if she had gone cannibal. Eating. Swallowing. Spitting, not singing at all. And she infected Jimi with her delirium. He smelled like some tree gone mad in a lightning storm. Breathing. He turned Teresa over and told her to sing. So she sang from her wicked throat. She sang words unknown to the naked ears of any man. She sang raving hymns with reckless abandon. Hymns of thirst. Their throats reaching into the mud. They prayed deep down into their bones. Cried out loud. Broke open the skies.

They found home in this, the silence of bodies. Teresa's thumb in Jimi's mouth. Thin flames burning under her skin. Pounded, she brought Jimi into the desert.

My One Night With God

In my body, God excited me with the torments of His silence before He even had the chance to touch me. My ribs rising and falling with all the mirrored pose of an innocent virgin beneath the place where the skin breaks. Propped up on skinny elbows I offered my throat. Bones pressed down into the dirt. This filth of God making his desires into speech. Word of. He hesitates. Trembles. About to put His body into speaking. Mary's last words, "Do as he says." My mouth. I merely begged Him to forgive me and to punish my longing for an eternal night. Under His eyes. To ease His anger, I gave my body over to His glorified body. Looking. Watching for the clouds to make their way across the sky. Slice the mad moon. He cut into my eye. A slice in my flesh for His nearly worn out fingers. This, my skin, made into the image of God from some lost dream. Mirrors cracked. I wanted for Him to show me my own wickedness. To carry me to the edge of some cliff. We stood in among sharp rocks. A sudden blow. Swollen. Tortured tears and God's hysterical lips on my lips. Lips. White feathers scarred with blood.

I longed to cut myself to pieces. To show my joy inside this desire for God's touch. For God to take me to the present moment, for His own desires to tear open my speech. A violence for speaking. God grew big inside me, so big, too big. Pain spilled with my blood into a river miles away. Memory and desire mixing. And God moving all over my body like there was no tomorrow. Like he knew something I didn't know. His revelations moved inside me. Each finger. Each thrust. Each tear into my skin. Through my flesh. He threatened that He would withdraw from me. My eyes dilating. His pleasure working inside me. Feeding on the body. Waking my body to thunder. Cotton mouth. Little boy with thoughts of becoming a lonely girl. Dry tongues stirred the roots. Still. Afraid to even smile. My longing for the desert. Deep, God, forever deep, penetrated me like he owned my wounds. Entered me again and again, prolonged my pleasure with slow, deliberate movements of his invisible speech. The kinds of words that only God has mastered. Made from the flesh. Into the flesh. One after the other. I was counting each and every move that God's hand made on my body. Counting. God snatched at my mouth with his mouth. Biting. Hunger. With a slight parting of His lips, God made it rain. Mud. God pushed my back into the mud. My ribs quiet and broken. Separated at birth. Hands on my shoulders. The sweat of God burned my eyes. All through my body, I smelled God, tasted His body and blood on my fingers. Spit words, the words of God, from beneath my skin, from somewhere in my bones. The wind cursed my desire, blew through God's hair. Alive through this, my body. I fixed my eye on his desire becoming. Give Him what He wants. My mouth opened. Red lips ripped apart with wanting Him to push me back down into His earth. Breathing did violence to my ribs. I choked on uttering a few sweet moans, not aloud, but inwardly, out of pain. God pulled me from my skin toward the light. Brought me into His bright silence.

I walked into my own book, seeking uncertainty.
This is the book you wrote.
And you are the woman.
I am.

Litany Of Our Body

For m

"It was as if no one had heard."

1. Confusion from Memory

Alice stood before me, beneath a cross carved from the dying wood of an olive tree. In the shadows, she forced me to suffer the disillusionment of her memory. Her loss of photographs. This desire to become desire. Near the edge of her jeans, the smell of history stains her skin. Our bodies being buried inside the space of forgetting. To forget forgiveness. Wet dirt, mud from her garden, covers her skin. Close to my mouth, I live with her scent, the smell of damp earth. A hunger that can't be resisted. Alice gave in to her own possession. Her need to return to the convulsions of her muscles. Her body craved this punishment. Wanted for me to deny her body. She wanted for me to turn away from her presence, for me to turn to the side. She lived in fear of her own temptation to travel. To follow her longing to disorient her body from home. "If I can come to be no longer familiar with home, to go on an ambiguous voyage with your body speaking to severed tongues."

In some dream, one that has recurred every night since her youth, she found herself walking near an ocean. In those mornings following these dreams, Alice wanted this ocean to deliver her, to enter her. If only she could dip her fingers into the wet spaces. To make wet the split of her skies. Alice clamored about inside her flesh trying to begin to move past this place of her will, into a space that allows for forgetting. She wanted little more than to forge her own vague idea of her desire into dirt and sky. To sign her name on the surface of the water. She had spent years sewing herself together with a desire for words. For letters of her body. Her tongue bleeds on words that suffer her saying between her teeth. Her tongue slips. Her cunt. Seven lonely days of hunger. A twisted magnolia tree falls, against God's wishes, to the dry earth.

Ragged men in orange suits knocked on her door one morning. They had come to cut down the near-lifeless dogwood trees in her yard. Careless men with their weapons. Men who cursed the sun. "I need to tell you these stories, Doug. The sound of their saw. The breakdown of my bone. I just called. I thought you might be home. I thought you would know. Would care." Without a thought. Her need.

She collapsed onto my fist. The scent of this woman, green leaves of California winter, stained my knuckles. She burned into my skin. The fire that cannot separate itself from the flame. "I fear staying will be too comfortable. Your shoulder." She saved a handful of white blossoms.

Your body. This body that becomes my body as I move. "How can a body forget?" Our bodies live in memory. A sacrament that marks our skin. She wanted to create desire, not need. Her breath on my forehead. I wanted her without this need. My own memory haunted me. Pulled me into the places of caves and corridors. I had forgotten the curses of tormented blood. "How can this body not know?" The damage of needing. Hers. Blistered skins boiled beneath the sun.

She becomes bored. She becomes perverse. Disguised words flee her throat. A body that turns against her body in words that fail. An escape route that duplicates her silence in a mirror that can no longer remember. Rivers of smoke beneath the loneliness of some breathing. This pain that some lover's kiss brings from beyond the grave. He is kissing, she thinks, this mouth, my lips, which has just been kissed by another. He kisses these eyes that have just looked into another's eyes with longing.

2. The Sacred Sleep of Language

"I am pulled toward your bones," she said, " to breathe in the place where your words come." But her words becoming language were always veiled. She wanted. Had this desire to come to speech. She longed to be invaded, then to be rescued from her own furtive secretiveness. Her words failed. Drifted away from her body. She dreamt of finding someone with kindness. But, day after day, she pulled back away before she dared to enter into the saying. To touch this body only through words.

Blood comes from everywhere. The dirt is blood of a different kind. Still. It is blood.

And to hear myself say her name. I run along the American River with her name in my mouth. Dry sweat of summer. She brought me the blood from between her legs, carried blood to me from the rivers. "It is not mud, Doug. The dark stains." The hard, black stains on the sheets. Stay with me now. Through my bleeding. Come. Cruelty is this coming to blood. To her blood. We dug deep into our muscles. To be beneath her body. This longing to open my legs. Her voice. "I'll read your skin like tea leaves with my fingers." I become her blind girl. This boy startled by her speech.

She opened her legs. Crushed with fatigue. Her body was possessed by an awful thirst too great to live here and now. She could only live away from herself in distraction on the edge of speech, outside of her body.

In the eyes of disenchanted angels, Alice seemed to had been changed into being merely a cut without the desire to bleed. The veins of her cold skin deep blue. Her mouth opened, red and raw. Speechless with numb muscles. My body, this body—my own way of seeing my flesh through her eyes—grew visible, locked inside my grandmother's dark cherry looking-glass. I longed to come near her broken twig. Her bent elbow a mix of roots and desires. Her bent elbow cracked my ribs. To lean my body into the flesh against the body of her body. I imagined that I could touch the inside of her. My hand through her skin into the inside of her wanting to speak. There. I found my body there. Alone. Uncertain of my own place. I struggled toward forgetting. So near her skin my mouth became agitated. We waited into the night, into the dirt, for the sins of these words. To create a language that experiences our need. Is this love or just some confusion of tongue. Parched lips. To live inside the desert without water.

I found inscriptions of rose petals on her skin. My hunger. Eyes that burn.

One morning, she walked through my window—the window I could see—in a dark manner. Through a glass darkly. This much I have known since those days of lost holiness. This pull toward the root. Her skin splintered on the floor. My urge to bring my finger to the space between her ribs. To press. To break into her bone. "In the beginning of coming to my body I have uttered words only to you. Only for you." These words in the making of words. I have held in my hands flowers that die during the rain season. Stood alone in the muddied waters of the Monongahela River. That thick sludge of metal desires. My toes sunk in the wet sand. Cold ankles. We stood in the slow river in the morning after we nearly killed ourselves with leaving. A faint memory of the Delta breeze. Shivering. "I am cold now," she says. Shivering with the same tremor of loss as leaves in autumn. Withered leaves detaching themselves from her body. Falling. The sensual epileptic fits of her memories coming to be present on her skin. But my tongue is empty, nearly lifeless, in my mouth. I want to warm her, so she would not be stranded. So she would not believe herself to be alone even while in his arms. The arms of some other without a word.

She lives inside me this girl. Has lived here inside me for years. I would shed my blood for her love. I breathe wanting to be a scar on her body. The one that she relentlessly claws. To be the scar on her cunt that burns her fingers when she touches. Reaches. I scratched my skin. Scratched and scratched my skin. I made blood come from my skin. Beneath my skin is the becoming image of this girl. I have seen this. Her cunt broke my skin. Into my bones. Her scent, the scent of Alice, lingers at the edge of memory. I seek to touch her scent. To enter this movement to water.

"A desire cannot be sacrificed. Desire is never burned at the stake." These flames enter my skin becoming bone.

I have not forgotten the house that we lived in then. What it is like to lie.

The part of me that is not there, she knows. She has given this to me in moments of strange carnality. Her meat and mine. Skin without speech. I could not take my fingers away from her eyes. We stayed locked in time for days without end. I watched her cutting apples. Cutting with a delicacy that I had never experienced before. The sound of the knife through the apple to the cutting board. She cleaned strawberries, deep red strawberries. The small strawberries between her fragile fingers. For this moment, I live inside a world of her gentle hands. She stared out the window. Her eyes, empty, looked away from her to the desert. "You don't have to live like this," I tell her. We could not hear the storm outside. The clouds coming over the mountains.

3. When Doves Cry (for patti)

- 102 -

Alice's body shakes. Uncontrollable shaking. Night after night, her body wrecked. Tormented by migraines and the endless deserts of insomnia. She travels wine dark seas never to come home. Seizures that cannot be tamed. Cannot be contained. The nuns of her boarding school want to hold her to the ground. Force her demonology back into the earth. Crucify her sweet body to the dirt. To make still her violent body. To force stillness onto her skin. This trembling girl with a mind of her own. But she refuses their hands. They want to medicate her with prayers, to carve salvation into her skin with needles. Secret vices behind the blinds. To cure her of her desire to speak from the depths of her womb, from the places of bleeding. They tell her to control her emotions. They warn her to settle down. To not talk so much. To not feel the world around her. "You make," they tell her, "a cross of your emotions."

Alice shoves her fingers deeper into her skin. Breaks into her own cunt. She travels through her cunt to some place that has never been known before. Her knuckles scrape hard against the insides of her body. The insides of her words. She prays deeper. But she can no longer breathe. She just wants to step into some desert, to allow herself to find the place of tears in her body, to weep. This beautiful noise. She takes my hand, pulls, pushes my hand into her. She becomes lost in this wet incarnation. The deeper she takes me the more she comes to know of saints and of deserts.

There on that inside she unearths the frayed languages that have been left out of the books on her shelves. To be near her books. If only to live my life close to her books. To hold one of her books in my raw hands. Books that she has destroyed with her own writing. Scratching out words that did not belong. Writing and writing so many words that no one could ever tell where one word begins and some other word stops. Words on top of words. Where her words become their words. Their words become her words. Her books flooded with all of her writing. Easy prey for flames. She had placed all of her words. All of her. Her. Inside these books. "I want to survive.".

Her fingers, she told me, were beginning to fade. To no longer be. The print of words, scars, on her fingers. We are these layers, Doug. Unspoken name, she holds his breathing silent in her mouth. She waits. More still than the moment when her body clenches. The muscles of her shoulders. Each breath a poetics of the sacred. "I have always known these languages. Have gathered them to my bones," she says. But she can say nothing more of this, only keep her mouth still.

Good and evil lie side by side while electric love penetrates the sky.

The nuns lose themselves. Nuns made blind by this gaze. The spectacle of Alice's writhing body. They pollute themselves with looking at her. Alice's fingers disappear inside. Her ache is a cut that refuses to heal, that cries no name. Changes color. If I could find one just word for this love. Sweetness and light, she stands on the edge of a cliff. Sharp stones beneath her feet and something white near the water.

These nuns feared the flames sent from above by the anger of a jealous God. Lightning that burns the dry bushes in the backyard. Fire that purifies our breathing. Before I knew any of the names for Alice, she licked my thighs. Her saliva. The soft dew of her mouth. I could feel her breathing on and on. I want my teeth to taste like her skin. On the inside. To surrender. Her mouth, desire lost in some wild forest.

4. The Scenography of Writing

Some days Alice nearly drove me mad with thirst.

Sitting on the steps in the hallway. Waiting. Rocking. Her body shaking, always shaking. Her hands shocked with her own faith, her own needs. To speak in the sleep of others. No love can be expressed between us. Love doesn't exist between us. The bone that becomes bone. The bone that stays inside the skin. Bones without words for saying. Under the skin with no silence. She waits for a promised sign. The anxiety of a lost rendezvous. This enchantment: to sit without doing anything.

The wet of her breath. Afflictions of the word becoming flesh stuck in her throat. Caught by the rough places that had only known saliva. No map. "I can't crawl to the surface," she told me one morning. The mud all through her. She had grown tired of living inside the mud. Even those days when she discovered some occasional stone. The kind of stone that comes close to being a pebble. The sort you carry with you from here to there. Over there. The stones that melted in her mouth. To savor each last syllable of the stone. I tasted this stone on her skin. In her cunt. I made this stone warm with my skin. My touch. This mouth. The pull of the mud was too much for her.

Her lips red and unforgiven. Her toenails some shade of pink I have never seen before. Her fingernails almost indecipherable but alive in the colors of longing. We were naked and did not know whether we had survived some terrible rainstorm or if we were dying in a warm baptism of wanting. Last night's blood had dried on the sheets. Neither of us could know where the blood had come from. This loss of memory. A full moon. A sore mouth. My thumb broken. Our hands disfigured but joined to each other. Her body tired. Her body awaited my fingers. This fist. Her body is a beauty undisguised. But this body meant very little to Alice. She wanted an act of love. One acquired through repetition. One that longed for the moment to abandon language. One that would force us to partially become each other.

***

All acts of love are demands that the body open. Split. Tear.
***

5. A Woman Between Mirrors

Alice looked away from me. She never stays. Pulls her body away from this moment. Apart from this place, the tear of my skin. Her skin travels into the lost forest. She drives away into the night. Disappears her body. This present becoming presence. She drives straight down the road without turning around. Going elsewhere. Already far away, invulnerably protected by flight. Alice is gone now. Probably gone for what will inevitably be forever. There is no way to measure this loss that moves to infinity. Only an empty gesture remained, a costume piled on the floor. Empty of her. My heart, a simple orphan's desire for a homeless loner to call me to come home to her. To live my life with this desperate girl among the debris on the innocent riverbanks. To call for me to come to her. "It is necessary," I told Alice, "to go to as many extremes as possible. To create these new lands. To disturb our own borders." The back of her knees. My mouth breathing into her skin. I caressed her arm, kissing the nook between her elbows. She had been in the sun all day. Feverishly hot and scented. June in Sacramento. Be with me tonight.

This girl with strawberry hair could no longer speak. Speechless girl filled to breathing with desire. Her throat. I wanted to tear the veil from her throat. The words let loose. To fly. In years past they wanted to cut out her tongue. To still her from thinking too deeply. To stop the emotions. Join us and sit quietly. Your ambitions are vulgar. Not part of this world. Naïve desires of an irresponsible girl. You should not ask for so much. Alice remained breathing on the inside of her body. My hand moves toward her shoulder. This home becoming lost. Trapped with wanting. The kind of wanting known only by those sleeping lovers trapped in fairy tales. Waiting.

She comes in rages.

Given and forgiven.

"I am broken and weak," Alice says. "Perhaps now in his kindness he will be strong."

Alice holds dear her desire for metal spikes. Her father, a railroad man, had worked with his precious hands until the blisters killed him. She wakes each morning with foreign cuts across her skin. She wakes without memory. Each day in the beginning. Word to flesh. She wakes to forgetfulness. Words in fire. Words without water. This desert where there is no ocean. The echoes of ancestors carved into her voice. She lives wanting to forget, to not return to her body. To move away from her becoming known to her body. To speak before herself in her skin. This desire she never says. Can only look away. Her mouth opens, but she can only wait.

"Why do you always cover your mouth with your hands?"

Alice held herself back from breathing. She locked her desire away from speech. Afraid some truth would fall out from her mouth. She held her breath to choke back the possibilities of words. To fight back against becoming language. The deep-rooted temptation to say. She held herself in. Body and word. Even her cough. A wall of thorns. As a child, she had cried over the despair created by the sudden end of a novel. Her privacy violated by the loss of the story. The spell broken by the departure of language. She cut all bonds when she read. Allowed herself to be carried away as if she were looking into a mirror. Her father, one time, had to whip her to make her stop crying over a story that broken her heart.

Alice could never lived in the place she was in. She is only driven by her need to recreate herself. To escape from one place of being to move to another. The quick changes of careless scenes. But sometimes the change was too rapid. Her movement in between worlds that she could never make into sense. It had become more and more of a struggle for her to end one role to become herself again. The other that she left behind, this fragment of herself, felt betrayed. Often fighting against her own rejection. An abandoned truth on the floor of some other apartment or house or street corner or hallway. Lately, she had begun to lose the original Alice in these constant transformations. Where had she gone? Ever? She could no longer remember her own self. To know her self from the inside. She could not distinguish her self from the performances of her self that she projected in dead mirrors. Every improvisation another loss of beauty. An absence of depth. Another day of moving away from her own skin.

"I can't stop being her. But I am safe with you. Here," she says, "You will be here. Home inside this stillness. The safety of your touch. You make room for me. I will no longer have to struggle. This, my refuge."

7. Forbidden Territory

Alice refused to allow God to be the only one that could make her bleed. "See," she whispered, so that God would not hear her, "I, too, can make my body into bleeding. My own bleeding." Body into blood becoming. She showed me her blood on the very tips of her fingers. "Skin is just a layer. I am beneath myself."

A lonely child, Alice wants to sit down in her bedroom. On the floor. She shuts herself inside her things. Things that she keeps close to her, in her personal care. These things are always there, here, inside her. She touches tiny objects that she discovers with her fingers. Touches them. Boxes. Souvenirs. She lives inside the corner of her small, cluttered bedroom beneath the window that opens to what is closed. Here she remains suspended. No clocks. No rulers. Nothing to measure time or space.

To be free. Here. Where she lives. One night I watched as Alice folded her clothes. Pulled lint from her sweaters. Tiny fingers nearly homeless with prayer.

"Not a word," her mother warns her away from speaking. She places her fingers on Alice's lips. Her father's hand over her mouth. The two silences, the two withdrawals. Not, a single word. Once upon a time. Of this, to anyone. Her father had disappeared. It is night. A moment from her childhood that she carries with her. Each day she remembers these punishments. "Your silence punishes my body. Don't." I have wanted for my life to make a story of my body inside the becoming of her body. To make a body of this story. Her body becoming my body becoming. Her bones held the secrets of innocence broken. I wanted to say I. Drowning in lost memories for her father, this father, from the days when forgetting was impossible. Her father goes to the ocean. Stands there until his feet become wet. He goes into the mountains. Nearly falls. He goes deep into the desert until there is no longer anything blue. Just red and orange. Burnt dirt.

"I think I heard a bottle, Mother. Something breaking."

"It was nothing, sweet girl. A dream. Go back to sleep."

Her mother sings small songs under her breath to Alice while her father slips away into water. Unheard.

All morning Alice sits at the breakfast table. A full glass of orange juice that she can only stare at. Her hands. She sits on her hands. The toast on her plate. She dreams of falling asleep along some road.

Let this pain live elsewhere. "I want the pain to travel down into my body. To not be here." She tries to pull the pain away from her eyes. Alice wants her mouth to be empty of this hurt. She wants to make visible markings of her desire to leave. Find a new place for this pain. She disbelieved in pain that left no bruises. Knuckles and wrists. She knows there is a knife in her drawer. One she had found in a ditch.

I look down at her pale wrists. Her small bones nearly invisible inside the white of my touch. Cuts, scratches, lacerations. Her acts of love. Thick and dark grease the mark of her vacant fingers on my thigh. Not my blood but the water of the serpent moves through my body. Nameless without a sound. She erases my skin becoming traces of bone gone mad in some late autumn thunderstorm. Faint diseases.

My waste of this skin. Her body leans. Blind hunger. She has survived something she cannot recall.

Years ago, while I was still a child, Alice had tied my body to a tree. She listed her instruments. Ropes, rusted knives. Wrists burned and twisted. Words from kingdom come. She bruised me, used thorny branches to open my skin and then rubbed bitter herbs into my wounds. Wrote the names of torture on the sidewalk in chalk. Salt in my eyes. She had held my eyes open, one at a time, and dropped salt from her mouth down into my eye. Burned my sins. Buried my skin. I saw her wanting. Looked into her as she looked down into me. The blood of locomotives, of looking glasses, of unopened drawers. Grandma Schmidt had left behind for the living three nylon slips no longer white, and her scent. Cedar wood. And something red. The smell of red. Going like mad and yes I said yes I will. Yes. Alice's look hurt me. My need. To live inside pain deeper than skin. But pain is no word. "I am trying," she says. "I want to hold dear this memory that slips away from me. My father took the lipstick off my mouth, but he didn't make it bleed on purpose."

To live without desire. Without regret. To live inside red becoming blue. Moist longings. "The woman who writes me writes to avoid me. She won't accept me. She denies me in her very writing. She thinks she can forget."

8. Elemental Passions

We live now in the same neighborhood. Down the block a few steps. A few letters. The way she walks across the earth. Her long, dark hair in the summer night. Subtle footsteps. We sit on a balcony, with summer creeping into our skin, and kill the pain. Maria's blood near the surface of my touch. Late into the night we walk these streets. In the darkness of Dog Days. The dry heat of August in Sacramento. We touch. Invisible hands. Hold each other so tight we nearly break. The weave of her ponytail in my fist. To pull. Her full throat exposed. Raw skin in a moment of hesitation before blood and word become one. Her with her music. She offered her singing to me in the smallness of her mouth. An incantation of desire. Each note a slight brush stroke of her mouth upon me. Her song possessed my body. I felt her embrace through me. Kissed on her lips this song, the legends of trees. The tiny delicate dance of her small feet. High cheekbones and pale skin. Maria takes me into this other world. One of slow rhythms. She sits at her piano. Long fingers. My skin taut under her hands. My hands on her breasts, her stomach, her hips. Dressed in her pale skin and dark hair, my fingers, precise as an eyelid, enter her lips.

"There is a terror in resembling others," she tells me. She had a fear of becoming contaminated by familiarity. I lick the places where her skin has opened. Terrible wounds that have seized her flesh. Wounds that have taken her to the edge of a bridge. Dark waters. I once imagined that my bones and muscles were made from the core of Alice's deepest desires. The places that even Alice was uncertain of. Unaware. The ones she could not know, not in speech. Could not give over to speech. The haunt of memories inside the longing to touch. To become this. *Tell me what you see when you look into there?* To become here with her. The menacing, never-tiring, presence of my body. I try with words to force my body into this present. To stand on a porch in Ohio before her and breathe her cunt into my blood. We walk into the forest. Kissing tears. Ripping off our clothes. Her hips. Even in the forests of Ohio, Alice swims. In Pittsburgh. In Seattle. Alice does not need an ocean to swim. Alice does not need water for her movement into her body.

8. This Silent Woman Slowly Parts Her Lips

During winter storms, Alice tells me stories of how words are not the same as cutting. Writing, your voice, is not living. Words, Alice said, are never enough. *I can't find my body. There.* Her throat scorned, scarred by pebbles and careless varieties of religious experiences. As a child she had ground her syllables. Nearly to kingdom come. Tortured her teeth with every word. Her mother used to tell her, "You'll chip your teeth one of these days with the ways that you go about trying to talk." Alice did not believe that teeth could be so fragile. That they could break on a word. She began hating words, despising each word she had ever spoken. She had used and been used too often by words. Their weight on her body. As if anyone using words could do anything, could be anything. Could cross the street without tripping. She had become fluent in all sorts of random languages. She used to say words that starved me. A rough beast slouching toward language.

"What if, instead of being ground to pieces, words were just forgotten about like some kind of waste that can no longer be remembered?"

Forget my words, she says. She begs. Wants us to go back into the past before she opened my words. Before she gave. Before she began to say. There is no past there. Here. There can be no past prior to words. To the making of words. She spoke herself into tomorrow. No future. The clarity of Greece. Bodies without words becoming tongue. We stood silent and broken. Our bodies torn into the present.

9. The Girl With The Mirrors

Alice smelled of a woman that I had known years ago. Some woman in the desert. October. But she knew nothing of memory. Only a vague ache. She could not hold memory in her hand the way she could hold the hand of her lover. But memory began there. The folds of her skin. Her scent. In the loss of meaning. The impossible names that we give to the past. A small breath. One she barely recognizes as breathing, as part of her body.

My living bones eaten by lost stones.

Thorns from a rose on her pillow. Her sheets marked by skin and muscle. I turn her wrist over in my hand and see the remains of her bleeding. "There is a sadness in your voice," she says to me, "that even the angels cannot heal." The marks of a frightened knife across her skin. In my voice. The jagged edges of a serrated blade. I bring to her a hyacinth. She smiles. She calls me her hyacinth girl. Alice's numb fingers through wet hair. My eyes fail. Stuttering tongues. A cold coming. I opened the mutilated songs of her father. This father lost in some forest. She becomes a field in the morning fog. I have never been this alone for words. As if my words must travel across time, year after year, until they come to her. Some nights when we lay in bed talking I felt as ancient as that savage she carried within her. Inside her. *I am burning.* She never spoke about that place. Her desire. Her father. Once I could only cry. Her hands near my mouth. The scent of the sun on her shoulder. Skin girl. I wanted to drown in this silence. To give myself over to the waves. "My scent will find you," I tell her, "and make your feet ache inside those tiny shoes." The sugarplum fairytales will break.

When she slept with anyone she had a fear of committing herself to deep sleep. She feared sleeping too soundly; she had a dread of talking in her sleep. She suffered a her need for continuous and quick improvisations of motivations even while sleeping. A sudden justification. Now she wanted sleep. Needed sleep and wished for absolution so that she might sleep deeply. To rid her body of her anxious watch of the night. To fall into childish sleep with utter abandon. Endless hours of staring up at the ceiling, a slow fan trying to move the dead air of Sacramento. Alice lay awake. Full-blooded. To pray. *Let him be kind.* This need of hers for kindness. While others prayed for wealth, success, beauty, power, Alice prayed for and lived inside a need for kindness. "What if all I ever find is violence and cruelty?" Even the word, the sound and the thought of it—cruelty—tore into her body. Into her. She could no longer remember this touch from my fingers. My voice. She had made me into a simple photograph. Static. One that could be controlled as she vanished herself.

She struggled to dream her way to Paris. This city of lovers where policemen smile at stolen moments of illicit lovers. Where taxi drivers never interrupt a kiss. But she had come to be too weary lying in this room with closed windows under the unforgiving light of a tiny lamp. So she reached for the words in her bed. The loss of words scattered in disarray. Small pins that break her skin.

10. The Tears Of Eros

Tears are the place of water. That place where words want. Wet tongues, forsaken, that seek sound.
She carried water to me from some lost memory. Years later, Caelia would bring blood from the rivers. Rootprints. I enter into myself with my eyes closed. Here are some flowers for

your bloody mouth.

The words of her mouth made manifest her longing to tear into my skin. To break. Words becoming water. Words staying water. I give this to her from inside the saying before I can say. *The story I want to tell.* Tears were nothing but traces for her desire to speak. Her lips become her will. A voice of broken pain. Silence that is so deep, so endless, that it can only become water. Marine lover. I never fear drowning when I am near her body in water. Spasms of agony. Terrifying and voluptuous, her voice becomes hoarse. Raw throat cutting into the air when she comes. She wants to die here in fits and trembles. Pain arrives before tears. Alice begins to teach me the subtle differences between stones and tears. Teaches me to burn the sorrow from my eyes. She taught me to use pebbles as a way for making the burn go away. Alice sees herself in the mirror, looking, a woman of tears caught between doubts and dreaming.

Anguish is the same as desire.

In the beginning. All these myths that have died. Murdered by hands uncertain of their own destiny. God knew nothing of beginnings. Only an apocalyptic hunger. No script for pain. *The origins of these beloved desires. If I could learn prayer, the prayer of quiet, she would banish me of all bodily things. Alice arched her body in the air. Her forehead and feet on the floor.* I wanted her to move me past the structures of tears. Into the world of being released, of never knowing anything for certain. No safe words. She slowly let her breath come from her mouth. A sudden snap of my muscles. Her bone cracked bone. Alone and silent for all these years.

And then the cut of her mouth. "I have torn," she says, "everyone who has reached out to me."

Since infancy, I have sought my body looking for you. Lost in my bones. The holiest of mistakes. Following leaves that blew down deserted streets. Feeling you in the becoming to speech. I chase this haunted desire to become exile to my body. Through your mouth with your tongue to make words. A house without windows.

Red doors. I see red doors painted black.

Alice gets under my skin with her colors. We never found our desires for each other. We only had color. The inside of her mouth red that turns into pink when she gets too excited. She pleaded with me to turn the inside of her mouth purple. To bruise. She released my wrists. On top of me she whispered, harder. Her voice cracked. Static desires. Her breath. To beat her until she could no longer stand to say the word. Two or three hours later, she was alone inside her body.

11. Splinters on the floor.

"Ecstasy," Alice once said, "is as unfinished, as perishable as a flower." She wanted the danger of touching this flesh but without rousing a heart that would bind her.

We had found each other beneath a magnolia tree in Sacramento. A treelined boulevard in midtown. Our wet bodies trapped in a freak summer rainfall. We had been invisible for ages. Bodies cut apart by time. Then, without warning, with no way of knowing, Alice pulled my hand from my rib. In the image of. Blood fell down and made the earth wet. I smelled her breath, stale from the weight of lost desires. Someone had hurt her in the years before my skin had come to her. Someone had left her. But she cannot remember any of this at all. Not even a glimpse. Cannot recall his hands. Only a tiny cabinet beside her bed made by the gentle touch of a man who then disappeared in the night. *I did not know him. He could not exist.* She is breathing. The taste of his ancient skin now reminds her of the futility of renunciation.

I wanted to place my body near to that of the body of

Maria. Her feet worn into the bone by wandering over desert sands. The wind. We looked into the sky. Red so much red. In the sky her body. Her thin lips. The hard light of precious stones through a tight slit in her eyelids. Where once I saw only darkness. Invisible skin. A reason to be beautiful. Her mouth comes to my collarbone and marks me with her longing. We stood there in the dead heat of late afternoon. The sun looked so old. We kissed with the weight of our bodies. Into each other. Hymns of luminous memory. We learned to love again. Here. A dark blue silence that we shared between our bodies. Maria says the word *mimosa*. "There are mimosas in my garden, Doug." A place where joy becomes so acute it hurts.

Once upon a time, in the days before beginnings led to narratives, my cryptic Alice chained me with all her will to a kitchen chair. Muscle and word. Forced me to think of ancestors dying at the cross. To take her scar onto my body. In my skin I forgive you these sins. I longed for her blood beneath my fingernails. I scratched her cunt. She placed stale bread onto my tongue. Near the moment of the cross. We sat in the quiet for three hours. Prayed for dark skies. Rain in the mouth of the thirsty body and blood of Christ. Swallowing her as she breathed. This tiny girl cut my clothes away. Scissors near my flesh. Held, my Alice, I, these scissors opened, close to my skin without speaking a word to me. In all my bones, knowing each one, I waited. No breathing in this my body. Carried my clothes with her straight through the looking glass. And right there before my very eyes, this girl, nails of her fingers, scrawled demotic desires into the becoming of my flesh. Our bodies moved over the sands of some distant desert. Toes barely touching the earth. Her persistent lips tore into what little remained of my soul.

I becoming invisible and unknown. The only mystery that remains is the unspoken word.

I am told that Alice is my addiction. This drug. That I

need to write my way elsewhere. To close this mirror. "Seal your heart from her neglect, Doug." Disembodied voice on the phone. 4,000 miles. I am here. Know this, that I can be here with you through this loss. I don't have to be in Sacramento, Doug. Here. Your voice. My voice. Our bodies. Hear our voices. She lifted me out of my broken skin.

Years ago we had said goodbye. More years pass. Days and nights of broken glass and hard floors. I stood in a gray parking lot in Buffalo. The brutal cold. Cold beyond cold. She had left already. A dry parking space outside a hotel. Yellow lines and slush. She had left to go home. Mile after mile of concrete. And I struggle to return for another fix. One more hit and I will be cured. In college, how we died and died for one more hit. Caked blood. Sore wounds. No sleep. The godawful sound of a lit match beneath a spoon. Heat. A smacked vein. Spanked arm. I didn't feel a thing. Those simple joys before words. A shot down into the blood. Desires of lost boys, young boys in flight. Hanging upside down with the noise. The girls on the sofa just watching us on the floor as our eyes light the sky. Kimmie climbs down to my body. Her teeth bite into my chin. "I could eat your tongue, Doug. If you want. Just say." I hardly recognize myself. I want to feel safer in the morning. Be there in the morning. When I want. Suzi puts purple beauty on the tip of her tongue. I open my mouth for her. This melting of desire into body. She slides the dot onto my tongue. I swallow Suzi's beauty with the innocent smile of an angel coming to see the first moment of skin. Let me in. I travel past the cattle into the land of the lotus. I feel Suzi's mouth turning me into a butterfly. We love our bodies with fists and metal.

In the night, I become afraid. The secret that I bear. That we bear. To ride her body into morning. Her hand across my belly.

We dream of the muscles of horses.

Fragile words that break on the dead leaves.

Alice's mouth opens. But she can only wait. All confessors wait, to catch the words and moods of others. A kind of benediction before her movement into remembering. We scrape our memories for an incident out of our past. Some walk, some moment when we thought we knew each other, some pain that rips right through our desire, some time when we held each other and did not fear what the world thought. Anything to hold this, our bodies, together here. *I am her loss. She is my map.* A sanctuary for the desperate. To sit with her on the floor. She wipes the corner of her mouth. She loved to read about flowers, rolling and savoring the names on her tongue: spiraea, cynara hellenium, primula, chrysanthemum carinatum, schizanthus, zinnia, narcissus triandrus. Strange flowers falling down from the window ledge. Fireflies exchange their dying spark. A moment of light before dawn. Joy gives way to pain. Still, I long to feel the creases of time on her skin. For her to lead me home. As she grows old. As she sits on porches. To be with her hands when the light is fading. Slowly I commit such desire to memory. But how can desire become memory? The future becomes the past before it ever becomes the present. All memory is only desire. The past waits to be forgotten. She was living on the inside before forgetting. Carried with her too great a weight of untold stories. This weight of memories. Ghosts that haunted her. She could not name the ghosts from her past. She carried with her, all through her, this impossibility of forgetting of experiences she could not yet understand, blows and humiliations not yet dissolved.

It was not a flirtation.

Alice was this incompletion of words. All this I felt for her in these bones. Beneath skin. The senseless loss of her speech.

In some alley. Rats, cocaine, and a stuffy nose. Her speech. Voices, stuck in mud, cultivated my passions. Our drunken sleep on a dead beach. A lost city inhabited by a cry. Our mouths gagged. Still we wander around the desire to speak. Our deep throats bound to abandoned buildings that have died. In my body I inhabit these buildings and pray. We stumble through a door left ajar.

She felt her bones fragile in her sandals. Overwhelmed by the danger of her own desires. Brittle and crushable.

We were no longer of the living. We had grown to be alive only when living by the skin of our teeth. Feeding off each other's bodies. Alice was unable to think of an appealing miracle, so we slept into the late afternoon until the heat of the sun disturbed us.

12. Loving, I Give Myself You

I want a sentence for my body. I want my body in a sentence. To be placed tight into this sentence. To learn the sentence of my body. To find a sentence that in the making becomes a resurrection. Our skin is language. We rub our language against each other. She just wants. "I desire you." I scrutinize the writing of her body. Search her body no longer afraid of the cause of my desire.

Her fingers between her teeth. Between her legs. Pulling her hair. She withholds language, not the words but the abandon that they evoke. She wanted her body to be taken over by the language of the French. *Ile des doux secrets et des fetes du Coeur.* The way of her tongue and saliva. The physical place of loss. Words come out of the depths of her dreams for saying. Murmuring memory. *I must be faithful. Sacred founts.* She seeks me out between words and things. Finds me. Turns away from my body. Our bodies becoming this mutilated communion.

Near the bottom of her saying a word from her body she becomes a spectator of her own birth. Body torn with the saying. Words that come. The sweat of her brow. Cracked bones, split hips. Like a photograph whose images continue to emerge. A painting in the state of hysterical movement. Over time, faint ghostly images surface on these paintings, on Alice's body, as evidence of a derangement of the senses. Of the painter's stroke. Origins of intention. Thought processes broken. Mistaken alternatives. Her beauty resides in this elsewhere. All the little boys not seeing this elsewhere. Unable to travel. Or frightened by her movement. Making words out of her body. She sent her tongue searching over the roof of her mouth. The scars left behind from the words that she had, once upon a time, said before matter. To say in matter, to breathe through her past. Too often, though, Alice violated her own mouth with her words.

A forgotten memory that Alice held dear to her. Someone's child with pain unreconciled. Alice had lost her faith in the ends of sentences. She stopped herself abruptly. In mid-air.

I would love her willingly. Using words that to this day remain unknown.

Alice could never ignore her body when she spoke. She insisted on keeping her body in the present. She refused to simply speak with her mouth and throat and lungs and vocal cords. Her body, even in the here and now, kept reaching back for the old languages. It was as if she were somehow raping her own flesh and blood, in order to unearth these languages that had been destroyed. She fought against her skin, in order to come to her languages of the past that she carried with her. In her body. She is inside her body even in those moments of speech. The moments when the rest of us disappear. She wanted to bring the trauma of her words to the surface. Muscles knotted up with spastic gestures and erotic manifestations of her desire for language. Language other than the language that simply floats in space. Her mouth ached. Many nights she went to bed with a sore throat after trying to write. To speak.

I want to live in a remote valley where the larynx is a sexual organ. A place where we can have sex by talking inside each other's throats.

Her voice in me. An overlapping of lacerations. Here. I wanted her to give me a sentence to swallow. Her thick cream down my throat. Spilled onto my chin. To stain my skin with speaking. To feed me her way of speaking from the inside. I begged her to break me with her sentences. Each cut signifying a lost word. We made promises with our saliva. One night she did relent and gave me a sentence of her own. From her mouth. Between her lips, the heat of summer. When Alice spoke her tongue knew of no boundaries. Our life together became one of her teaching me these words from the inside. New words foreign to my mouth. But these words were always too strange in my mouth. They acted like a disease and I became a foreigner. My words becoming an inflection. Creating a mystery of my own speech. I could not hold them in my body. They refused to stay settled. Each word filled with her cracks. Broken. None of them smooth. Her words made my body uncomfortable. She had to force them into me. False and strange her words infected this body. I. Before she left. Before she began wandering, she tortured me with her silence. Her deep unwillingness to speak. Her body became an object. A place for her to survive the wounds in her skin.

13. The Virtue Of Her Tongue In My Theory

Tie me to the bed. Tie me down. I want God to want. I want God to see. I do not want to sleep. I do not want to eat.

I shot her up with amusing amphetamines and waited. I stared at her absence. A blind narcissus. God passing through. Sight unseen. I closed my eyes and Alice screamed.

A voice has no way of knowing its beginnings. A voice

can only interrupt, never begin.

I was lost inside Alice wanting me. The fear of hovering too close to Alice's mouth. She had in infancy discovered every technique for the making of me into a delicate woman. Her thighs knew all about the ways of nature. Her electrocuted flesh burned my belly. Arrested my tongue, Alice, between her blistered and burning fingers. It was spring and I could smell the dogwood trees in the air. The hard earth of April. Cruel. We walked down to the Monongahela River. Splashing water on our bodies. Hanging from trees. Fingers chilled. She put my hands in her pockets. Alice's tongue, my tongue, I am tongue. Split. I am becoming only a struggle of bone and flesh interrupting the dirty languages of what appeared to be merely my backward glance. Caught, said she, looking.

You have to find the place of sacrifice.

Alice's unvirgin sex howled against the looking glass.

Her breath across the mirror like she was never there to begin with. *I have to start you off with fiction. Such is your heritage.* She ridiculed the lonely boys of the neighborhood who looked and looked but dared not speak. Closed mouths. Lips locked. Zipper desires. The first time I pulled the zipper of her jeans down. Her tight jeans. A second skin. It was as if I was opening her. This cunt. Hers. I.

In the simplest skin, Alice became trouble near my throat, thick and unfamiliar.

I needed her mouth to come to know my skin. Choking on words. Our desires drained the rivers of water. Silences passed inside the in-between breaking us. She traveled. She began moving her body away from my breath. The sun going down. Slipped her body into the earth. My mud girl. Stained skin. She wiped her lips. Disappeared.

In the morning, she told me stories of how her body felt beneath the body of the body. This longing to know her father.

This father who worked making tiny furniture with a touch as light as a cobweb. Restless buried memories. Each morning, memories that she could not control. Tinkering, her desires, with my broken rib. Of her dreams. Nightmares loose and rambling. Her movement to trespass. Hands beyond the places marked by rose petals. And I held my breath. Bit my lip. Beneath her becoming. Teardrops. These thighs. Broken surfaces unknown to our eyes. She forced me to open my uncomfortable flesh. We searched for the desert. In her youth, Alice had threatened to take my voice into the desert. She promised we would go to Greece. And once there I could find the taste of the sea in her mouth. We could sleep with water, hear the sound of water with our bodies.

This.

It was the room growing tighter around her.

But I could no longer think.

You think she understands any of this? Could. To move into movement.

This is her body in my body. This is my body becoming her body. When I see her body I find the places that I have rejected in my own body. Becoming. Written in the old languages. The languages that have been buried in sand. Our love was born together. The mystery of a sad smile. Every word a change in syllables. No word twice in our mouths the same.

Take your fingers out of your mouth.

And now Alice, in the name of a sound heard in the wilderness, began to teach me skull-fucking. Taught me her throat. Her cunt. The smell of ancestors going to sleep in the forest. She taught me the smell of metal. While I was distracted by her scent, she recorded my voice and stuck it to the surface of the mirror. The pink- and blue-tinted obscurity of dreaming. A drowsy language like that of birds and flowers.

I saw my body turning into language.

But why is she here?

She watched me with her. Our reflections driven into the mad place of dead roads. Knuckles. There is more speech inside Alice's knuckles than there is inside her mouth. In the mirror, I nearly saw myself looking. Our bodies began making our way of touching into uncertain emotions. I doubted her body was actually in the mirror. She did not bleed in the mirror. Her body bled onto the floor. Something began happening to her skin in the mirror. She had lost history inside her body. Kneeling. I knelt there at the very tips of her toes. Her belt. Every move into my bone another memory. Hysterical fluids flowed out of her speaking into my desire to want to become down on my knees. Alice's half-hidden teeth in my unspeakable flesh. Suffocated my saying. Her orange blood from me, driven by slanted desires. Broken tents. Pink against the white of her thighs. "You know about broken tents. The blood of those tents, Doug, to take that blood into you. To carry my bleeding with you."

I recognize her.

She began the inscribing of familial memories ripped out of these muddy riverbanks across the deserted photo albums of white eyes. *Be careful, Doug, or I will finger your eyes.* I kissed tears from her eyes when we were only children. I looked at her. Tasted each tear as she squirmed her body over the earth. I seemed to be eating my own memories. This is mud, she told me. Mud of our bodies spilling into rivers. Taught me in words to stand in the rain. Cold spring rainstorms of the Midwest. Rain cutting into our skin. Taught me how to make mud. Skin is not mud, she said. Told me, skin is skin. And we could never talk of skin.

Only this.

And she put her skin near my skin and we breathed. With her nails she dug me up again. Brought me to this other surface. Above the water. Into the dry heat. She told me, under cover of slow breathing, that my veins were made for cutting. That God knew that I would come to bleeding. At birth, God had given me bleeding. With her. "In the desert," she said, "there would be sand and our blood. The sky." To enter the kingdom of tiny thirsts with her. This happiness of not knowing where I am going. And after bleeding to return to the ocean.

Accusations and afflictions of the word.

"Some part of me tears off like a fragment. Fragments that flee from my own sense of myself. This desire. I lose vital parts of myself. A part of me pulled to this or that man. A part left in some hotel. Alone. A part is drawn into a book. One that has not yet been written. The books I love so deeply, unwritten but scribbled across pages of scrapped paper and glossy magazines. A part of me pulled out of me to my family. This smile I practice day in, day out. Someone will take my place. My punishment of myself. Where I am, I am in many pieces, not daring to bring them all together. To be here where I will not be hurt for a few days at least."

She whirled about in a tiny frenzy without devotion to any sorrows. Her voice a torment of contradictions: she read little fairytales in this voice late at night while in my arms. Repeated each fairytale until I began believing. Then her voice disappeared each tale. The flowers she wore wilted. Her presence, soft and vulnerable but fleeting.

I look into her.

But she has vanished. The mirror cracked. She had come to an end of herself. She was just passing by on her way to some other place. Another life.

Desires to live the life of the desert. Writing. Thigh-to-thigh. But Alice knew nothing of deserts. Never once. This body meant to be near my body. I. You. Your body in my body. All these years. This body – sometimes I thought that Alice wanted me to kill her—into my desires. I am this sister to God. I know that I am not her. Flesh across the floor. I am not here. Words across open spaces. The outlines of my desires fractured by rumors of her despair. Her need to move. To travel.

She had escaped danger for just a day, that was all.

In the morning, Alice was no longer present. Some lost presence. An inappropriate photograph. An inaccurate realism. I look in the mirrors. Search the corners of the rooms. I look in the dust. I lick the sheets of the bed for a taste of her skin gone. To leave traces is forbidden. We burn letters. Notes. Erase tapes. Needing is a mute touch of offering a hand across empty spaces. Fire ants bite into my flesh. This flesh not forgiven by God. This flesh Alice thought she knew. This flesh Alice fled. This urge to remember a sense of bodily anguish. I lie still before the moment of speech. The restlessness of sleepless nights. The corpse of her memory rotting inside languages that can never come.

Their love signifies that neither can see the being of the other but only a wound and a need to be ruined. No greater desire exists than a wounded person's need for another wound.

—*Georges Bataille*

After Skin: Words That Come

By lidia yuknavitch

dear doug,

      *you have broken me. I suspect you know this. under skin,
saliva, my mouth was never mine. Never. When I entered your text
I was of course undone. Obvious. Stupid to say. Trying to say. You
are everything I have given up on, and thus, I am ravaged and
made primal. Just a body. Then I look back at that sentence, "just a
body," and I think, isn't that everything? That sentence? Your rib
cage against my rib cage. The cavities of your geography, hills of my
flesh. Your neck. My jaw. I'm crying right now again. Forgive me.
this is too much to try to write about so much I feel I shouldn't say.
This is the house. The rose lips of a child. I'm not in the habit of
being present. I thought I could live in art. You have broken me,
you always have, you always will. Don't tell me you can live in
ordinary ways, because I won't believe you, ever. I didn't think that
words could do this. I knew they could give me mobility, a home, a
secret naming, a body. I did not know they could touch.*

ever,

lidia

ANTI-OEDIPUS

When I grow up, I will be stable.
When I grow up, I'll turn the tables.
—Shirley Manson

A schizophrenic out for a walk is a better model than a neurotic lying on the analysts' couch.
—Gilles Deleuze and Felix Guattari

Language Cuts

Writing about Rice's prose is akin to performing a skin graft operation. Yet as the material at hand lives and breathes beneath our fingers, the attempts to isolate, cut, and grasp leads to the realization that this epidermis has no definable boundaries. Moreover, it seems to thrive on teasing our desire for comprehension.

The skin formed by Rice's text surrounds a vulnerable center of raw flesh. As he cuts and scratches into his sentences, layers peel away, grow back together, breathe, fester, bleed.

Reading across this surface shows why some of its components had to be wrenched from their deeper contexts. The words often hover, reeling back from painful contact with the raw flesh beneath. If some of his narratives were to connect cohesively, their seamless embrace would bring the painful center unbearably close.

The pores, when opened, offer an exit for desire, bewilderment, anger, and emotions often pushed aside by palpable grief. Rather than cranking them open, Rice sculpts these fissures into viewing holes. This process is at the core of his art. Gashes heal into textures of unbelievable softness. His blisters become tender to the touch, and in the surprise of this sensitivity, beauty comes to light.

It is through a sheen of beauty that we see, "pinned and wriggling," the raw flesh, electrified by the dynamics of familial relationships. The history of father/ sister/ lover/ grandmother/ otherself is reflected in microscopic gleams, crevices caused by pinpricks often sharp enough to set us reeling. This skin, with its manifold lacerations, its smoothness marred by melanoma where the voice seems fatally psychotic, is one we want to touch.

I could not compare Rice to other writers. That is why I

return to him. He stands alone, his voice so original it occupies an entire island somewhere in far exotic waters. Reading him, I remember diseases invented by the writers discovering new continents.

—Julia Solis, translator, editor/publisher of *Spitting Image*

Because the Night

As a child I often awoke in the middle of the night startled by the noise of blood breaking my body. Found myself lost inside burning dreams, walking across the sands of the desert. Footprints dead in the wind. Strange fingers pressed hard into my temples. I refused to believe in any of this. This, my body. The stories told behind locked doors. Whispering ancestors from the old country. Hungry to be yours. My bare legs streaked by the cold air of winter in Pittsburgh. This mistaken tongue began, without words, searching for the derangement of some other body. Unfaithful words spoken aloud from my mouth. Words, refused by gods and demons, thrown out against the dark into strange bodies reflected on the bedroom wall. In one corner I saw God standing in fire. Silent. Among flames burning all memories of books. Of the word in the beginning made flesh. The dust of God's breath. Apples that have fallen from a golden bough. A return to the Garden. There, I saw God. Without breathing. His awkward elbows and jaw. An open invitation to my own mortality. My legs parted. My lips.

In the beginning before the flood of language, my blunt fingers explored this body, mine, which I had been ordered to ignore. Curious about the torn skin at the precise moment when I came to know that God sees all and follows me. Into the attic. I climb wooden stairs. God leaves me there forsaken. I believe I feel my father place his hand on my shoulder but I only see a reflection in the mirror of some dear dead memory. The stories the mirror tells in silence. Feel his cold body close behind me. His gray hand trembles against the beauty of the mirror. My belly warm and soft. When I try to move, the ropes tighten. Into me. My father cries. Spilling blood and skin onto the hardwood floor. I fall down on my back. The weight of God holds me to the earth. Paralyzed in time. In some countries this is the sign for the awakening of love. My thighs like the threat of open scissors. My lips tremble. Speak, why does he not speak? So much dust.

I was taught to fear monsters under my bed, bogeymen in the walls, and angry angels hanging upside down from the ceiling. "They will," Daddy told me, "bite off your toes and toss them into the Monongahela River." Tales for a sleepy boy. Mother flicking and flicking the light switch. Three times. Me begging her to turn off the lights. Be done with it. Enough with the mythologies, the stories half-forgotten from the dead lands. The ones our ancestors fled, the ones without trees. The tales that never end, only begin. She stood in the shadows of the doorway and chewed away at her nails. Between her teeth. Pulled them off her fingers. Spit them onto the floor. In the morning my feet bleed. "The monsters will carry you off to hell," Mother warns me. "In hell, you can't ever be a girl."

I mistake mirrors for doors that have been left ajar.

Deep through these godless nights into mornings riddled by junk madness, I keep my eyes open, wide-awake. In stillness, not a breath, not a word of this to anyone. God made these shadows in the image of a lost soul. I wait, never to speak for my father to come home from work. Every minute, every night, I wait for my father. He with his body uses his body. The one God had given him at birth. In the name of his body, he interrupts my isolation. He takes away my weariness. I never cry. Not once. I never shed a tear. He likes that about me. I have heard that others have died because of their tears. Wet words from inside the broken promises in flesh.

Eleven years old. Late winter of 1968. The naked throat of a little child. Frail bones that hunger for hope. Cracked lips dry and peeling. It has been said that I was born choking. A rib broken loose. Indeterminate beginning. Not of this world. Not into this world. I come when I hear her beginning to speak. Words are her only way for breathing. She stands on street corners. Talking. Word following words. Chasing one word after another into another. Reckless and random she has forgotten all about breathing. Words, only words. Hypnotic throat girl singing of her body caught in the trappings of water. I wander in her voice through her skin. She carries me with her, body and soul. Steals me away from God. Alice draws me to the country of gray birds. She has become my sister of stone. I see her eyes like no other. The human torment of her eyes. This wanting.

I want to touch her like no other.

These guilty lips, mine, opening, stuck inside prayers of becoming a girl. For my father. So that he need not use his fists so often. So that his anger is more quiet. More gentle. Touch and let me touch you. I offer him each desire of my body past before I had become known as a boy. To be called a boy in speech. Inside speech that can not wander. She calls me her infant. But that is a dream, or it is years later and we are in some parking lot in California. Her teeth are in my collarbone, but this is my father. Now. I lay me down to sleep. Each night I lift my voice, whispering up at the plastic flesh of Jesus nailed to a wooden cross. Forsaken body of childhood. Grace of the Savior, my father. Without ever having been told of him, I came to understand. God warned me to be more careful. When I felt him inside me. I hesitated. Looked for a window. A way into the forest. He enters me. Blind God. Vague, abstract, uncertain of his next move.

In his arms I want him to hurt me. To beat my disobedient body into sudden desires and thrash my soul into some unknown language. More. To want more. His knuckles in my blood. In the image of. Stained hands and cold knees. I hope to be left alone on some riverbank. Discarded. Abandoned beneath a bridge on the Southside of Pittsburgh given over to the circle of homeless drunks sitting around their garbage can fires. Their warm hands lighting my flesh.

The burning prayer I cannot say.

God asked me to put my hand on my heart.

His lips on my lips her lips I remember. My back pressed into the bark of a tree. Pray. This flesh, mine, my soul to keep, haunted day and night by stunted freaks and biblical plagues. Locusts near my eyes scratched their way into my dreams. The Lord. Never, Grandma warned me, again and again, never look directly into the open mouth of God. If I die in the eyes of God before I wake. Apologize. Say it. The need for redemption. You must. Say this, the cutting of your body, into words. My sore mouth close to the feet of Jesus. A droplet of wounded blood, perfectly round. Forgive me, Son of my father. Pray without cutting into your skin through your flesh the Lord. No. I do not fear the boys in the neighborhood. The ones spitting on street corners. I only fear displeasing you. My soul this pain inside this place. Here. To take me into this dream where I can move my body across water.

Every single night small men with dusty skin sneak through my bedroom window, wake me from nightmares, from God's breath with their mad tales and pointy fingers. Seven screaming horses reciting stories about mothers relentlessly asking questions. Their voices, pain escaping from the shadows. Breathing their voices into my bones. I could not see myself dressed in these clothes that I had stolen from inside a looking glass. Borrowed woman. Drunken nights spent on a boat. I never did come to know their names, to understand how they had traveled from the old country through the forest. Just one more lonely night. Pinned and wriggling on the wall of a sawdust hotel. These men with their uncontrollable betrayals mixing memory and desire spoke in tongues of a world out past Babcock Boulevard. Carried rumors to me of a land that was somehow not Pittsburgh. Me, silent and still, in my barren bed all-alone filled with waiting. Glow-in-the-dark familial lines of blood being worn away by the passing of each minute. My mother's alarm clock on the night stand breaks into my bones. One by one. This rib then another. Ticking my body into a nightly ruin. My all alone, nearly dead eyes, squeezed shut. Infected desires of my body unable to forget those foreign fingers pressed into my neck. Those tiny men plucking my eyelashes.

Because I wanted no one to see me.

Each morning, my eyes inside a pain of not wanting to see. Cramped muscles. Hot and hard. Tendons torn out of joint. All night long. And I wanted to be entered. Dreamt of being entered the way any woman can be entered by any man. With the passion of Jesus wandering through the desert, I tried to push my eyes back into my soul. Push my eyes so deep down into the inside of me that I would make myself into becoming blind. Wordless. Invisible girl in this decayed bed. The bed that my grandmother escaped from sometime in the late 1970s. She had fled, screaming uncertain names, into the forest. Words flung loose from between tight lips. White knuckles. I stared up at the disappearing white of the ceiling, watched as God turned against Satan, the teeth of Eve through the skin, believing that, if I looked hard enough beyond original sin, then I could lift my body right out of my bed through the ceiling straight into the sky. My hands balled up into tiny fists. Frail fingers and prayers. Shouts into the street at a disappointed God.

Parasite girls in the far-off and long-ago tugged at my lips.

Sheets held to my chin. This throat, my memory of speaking, raw and empty. Without a scream. His desire, mine. Alice's fingers close to the secrets of lonely eyes. Bodies in motion but never in flight. Perpetual motion. Once she had told me that bodies at rest are compelled to remain at rest until another force acts upon them. In them. Break me open. The other side her mouth. The making of her will. Her forehead cracked the light. Wanting desire. Quiet.

Every night forgetful neighbors prowl around the shrubbery in our backyard, try to steal glimpses of my body through the window. My mother wants me to say in words why these neighbors circle our house each night, fumbling around, kicking the dog, waiting their turn. She wants me to explain my mouth to her.

The meaning of life: to take it in your mouth.

Swallow. Those without names. Speechless men in polyester.

Men laughed opening my eyes.

Close to dying. A death deeper than any darkness visible.

My mouth the slum of your desires. You break my teeth with your lies. Cut the corner of my mouth with a knife. You are that big. I lift the blinds, stare outside at these neighbors. The ones with all their eyes, trapped, looking in at me. Blinking through the blindness, I search their bodies for signs. The window locked shut. My mother seals the inside and the outside of my window with fresh caulking every day and night. She checks the nails she has hammered into the wooden frame of the window. Making certain that the window could never be opened. No air. Just to breathe. A breath. Outside, leaves moving. Concrete. The twigs of trees like the scratched bones of my soul. Soiled underwear. The mud of the river of my father.

I keep my knees locked together and beg God to find my body unharmed. Forgive me my fingers. My belly warm beneath. Rising to his touch. Skin ripped through by the beginning, in the making of desires. He kicked me and kicked me. Until I relented. The tight curl of my body becoming open.

He wanted to drown in this silence. To give himself over

to the waves.

I smell you on my body, Father. I say my word against your suffering. Try to make noises. I say your name. You refuse to hear my voice. Under your mouth. Say my name. You, then, enter me like a clumsy foreigner seeking a new home in unfamiliar streets. Your desire penetrates me here and there and here, again and again, until my own name becomes incomprehensible to me.

His body becomes a flame. Burning the skies.

Every night my father dreams. Sometimes these dreams make him speechless. Cut into his tongue. Red with white desires. Confused by pink kisses. A woman is forced to eat page after page from some cheap paperback novel. Her mouth is then taped shut and her throat is sliced open. She is left to die alone in some airport in Italy. This intersection. To travel. This woman disappears. She slides down a white wall. She goes out of the frame looking. Another woman, younger, runs down a hallway. A hallway without walls, only sheer curtains. Her white nightgown makes her body nearly invisible. We know that she will never be born, only die. Moonlit curtains.

Behind the rosebushes my nose bleeds.

I have been forced to remain silent. Begin my prayers all over again. My father is a phantom becoming his own dreams. Knuckled and rheumatic fingers. Quiet mornings listening to the radio report the weather, traffic, sports, news. My mother stays in the darkness, moves from room to room, turning on every light in the house. Even the flashlights. The nightlight in the hall. She stops and watches out the window. Waits for the ice cream vendor. The laughter of neighborhood children. My father's eyes floated over to the television set. Pulled into the bright light. The light.

My father sits at the kitchen table sweating. The dead of winter and still my father sweats. Nearly dies twice from heat exhaustion. The groundhog sees his shadow. We bow our heads. Six more weeks we must stay in the house. I can feel my father looking at us. One of us will have to pay. I spill my milk. Shaking hands that tremble with the desire, the need for flight. My sister starts counting as if by counting she can travel. Fingers, hands, toes, feet, the silverware. The letters in her cereal. She counts and counts but nothing goes away.

Day after day, now, my sister stays alone in her bedroom. She has locked herself in. She is no longer one of the family. She has abandoned hope and become an invisible memory. Divided by two. Tin soldiers and Nixon coming. In the summer of 1979, she burned all her books. Said she would become a vegetarian mathematician with an attitude. Would disprove every single idea that Einstein had ever conceived. E=mc2, my sweet ass, she said every single night at dinner. My father would slap her across the face with his hard bones and make her go to her room for the night. Running down the hall, she would scream that she, from this day forth, would only have sex with animals. Only consent to wild, senseless fucking. Sudden and random. To make her mouth into a gutter. To become a weapon against her sense of self. Her soul. To wreck her body. To destroy the very core of her being.

At night, this father's body became another anonymous encounter with my flesh. Just one more lonely night.

I waited. Nothing to count. My forehead is tired.

The dried, flaking skin of my fingers. Rotten flesh. Have you ever touched me in the winter? The miracle of her fingers inside my mouth. But she looked away. Picked at the bark of an old tree. For a long time I have been frightened of the uncleanliness of my father. I am impure. I say, "I am impure." My body, I longing for one warm night. One night of sleep. A way back inside where she forgets who I am. The dark room where there are no lights. Nails, inherited from ancient women driven mad against the moon, and from sons of fathers without speech, cut into my palms.

I live inside this house of silence where no one breathes. *Not a word of this to anyone.* My voice joined those of the ventriloquists in the attic. But once there had been echoes. Noise from the streets of history. On the other side of windows and mirrors. Persistent memories locked inside some lonely cry to angels or deserted flesh against the walls in some back alley. Left in that alley without a crumb trail. Nothing to follow. No way back home. The policeman, armed and ready, look into that alley at me. Watching. Waiting for me to make my next move. Hands and boots alert, waiting. Men in shirt sleeves lean on windowsills with all sorts of things to say about the Promised Land. Sauerkraut and kielbasa. Rotten beer and cigars. Visions of heaven driven by the desires of round stomachs and yellow-stained t-shirts. My father gets me drunk again. Old men in the shadows stare out at me. To give up my sexual habits would mean I'd have to discover some other means for tormenting myself. I bend into becoming their image. Made in their image without a thought.

"Look into my eyes little boy."

"Come."

I try to forget my name. Blisters. Cold sores. A mouth alive with pain. I can barely unzip his pants. The scar on his thigh terrifies me. He stands solid. Unmoving. Not even flinching. Smokes a cigarette. Dreams of anyone but me. I keep thinking that he will fall over on top of me. That he will die. Or that I will die. But he just closes his eyes. Continues to dream of nights at the movies. And neither of us seem able to die. My knees hurt. Stone cold heart of gold. We go on living as if nothing is happening. His pants at his ankles. Young boys turn their pockets inside out and shrug their shoulders. Brilliant colors in the palms of their hands all on fire. Offerings from nearly dead street gods. Yellow jackets. Purple dots. Black beauties. Christmas trees. Green spiders. Seductive tiny, pale blue pills. Gold ecstacy.

I buy a stairway.

Look left then right. Always look left first. Grandmother logic from the old country. Knock on the side door to the Piano Bar. These, my winter fingers, pick at the open diseases of my infant skin. Cook up some damaged dreams. Mad bubbles boil on a narrow, tight spoon. The needle takes on an eloquent life of its own. I tap a nearly invisible line. A shot in the skies. I ride a white horse that feels like heaven. Another lost angel. My eyes burn white. Red scars. Infected memories rush through my body. Helene touches my skin for the very first time. Her small hands unbutton my difficult shirt. She wants to experience the pain that comes with desire. She wants me to neglect her. Her forehead on my ribs, the weight of her sins. She unbuttons her own jeans. The waiting.

Rashes of my spirit.

Blood and blood. Skin of skin. Twisted hands.

I cried beneath this desire. My way for walking down streets forgotten. This body that stumbles.

I will not move from here until you have restored the inside of my throat.

My fingers I dip into the Holy Water. Receive communion down into me with loving you. Small lips opened and waiting. Interrupted by kisses. Each night more desperate than the night before. "Just one more time," I hear him say. I cover my mouth with my hands. This will be the last time. Try not to breathe so much. Afraid I will awaken God. If only for some water. If only some water beneath this red rock. You will become pure again. My skin dried by the sun. Rocks. Rubbing. Toil. He pulls my hands away. Holds my wrists in his hands. Down. Holds me to the bed. I relent. Give over to him his wanting me. He bites me. Smiles. I hear angels. I hear psalms. I woke up in love this morning. Went to sleep with you. The Partridge Family. I can't stop hearing.

My father has ten fingers.

February 3, 1966, my father had a fever.

My father wears Brute Aftershave.

November 22, 1963, my father dreams that I am a girl.

Let me forget. To be given amnesia. I try to will myself to become a deaf mute. To be left on a street. His cheeks fleshed. I was made to look. To keep my eyes wide open. This bed was too hot. The world had caught on fire. Turned yellow against the blue of my longing to be going. To take to the road. To find a road. I entered into a dream red with crying, a wilderness where screams were merely rumors brought from some other land. But I was unable to lift my body. I prayed for my muscles to take my body from this. From the here, this place.

A great beauty, like torture, burned my throat.

I could hear somewhere my only begotten mother breathing. Her child. Oddball woman, this mother lived the life of a stranger to my blood. A woman unknown to me. A deaf woman off in the distance. Always forever standing in the door-way but never once entering my room. Frozen eyes. Nothing better to do. Watching. Silenced lips cursing my birth. Dry mouth. Moving her feet against the carpet. Static electricity with no place to go. Her soul lost in the colors of some forgotten desert. Misshapen words. A veil of secrets invisible to the naked eye. Crippled mouth knowing only the lies of alcohol burning her bed. Told me once upon a time I would never be a girl, a real girl, the kind men die for.

I creep down the hall. A hallway so dark that each time I walk down it, I suffer beneath the joy of amnesia. Forget my name. Forge my skin. The smithy of his desires. Connect noth-ing to nothing. My sister, not me, trying to say I. This is my body to follow the will of the Father. Once my father made me sleep in mud. Rain. God makes it rain and the earth turns into mud and me unlocking the door I enter the house. My body leaves marks behind on the kitchen floor. A trail made of God's soil.

I am present to myself.

Wet. Footprints. Toes in the carpet. In my sleep, I open the door of my parents' room. I always wanted to be a good girl. Steal my father with a whisper. Take him away from my mother's body into the shadows with promises of kisses. I drag him through the dark corridors and up onto my bed. Pull off his clothes. And he begins the punishing of me for having eyes too much like my mother's. My hands on his back. There is no light of day. Just to be locked inside this. I feel my strength. Without asking forgiveness. Call on my fingers to dig into his skin. To open his skin the way my skin is open in the rain. To die with his red blood under my fingernails. The remains of his presence. My evidence of him. To swallow him. His cum inside me.

So my body will become a witness.

So this body, my deaf desires, will speak.

He confesses to me and I turn into the moment of his need. I throw my head back like any girl would. Like I have learned again and again. Tossed scraggly blonde hair. Blind ancestors. Holding tight his strong body. Desire in my hands.

Gave me his love and my hatred.

I rub my lips. I rub these lips. My lips. I rub my lips. Wild and free. Fear. Keep silent as before and as before that. There are no stories of my silence. I catch my breath. Hold still. Wait. Skin. My eyes burn. "Salt words," Grandma called them. The desires of the body are tears. I shed these tears, onto the hard floor, wanting you. In some other life she told me there were rumors of maps. Told me that concrete was not impossible. My eyes drifting. Out of me. Follow the white lines. Across the mirror I breathe in the mad suffering mysteries of angels. Drag the angry burn into my blood. Teresa and I call it bone-surge. Away from me. I look away from all that is happening to me. Searching for roads, paths that lead into the woods. Dull morphine desires. Wanting. Want. Something.

I stare into my open hands, her blood, and try to remember desire. She had bled onto my fingers. Fleshed forehead in dead heat. Spit from my mouth, from someone, on her skin. Ashes of my mouth. Mixed with the red of her cut. I put my lips to the center of the palm of her hand and kiss her blood. My body feels dry. Or I feel my body is dry. Broken wrists. The back of my head against the wall.

The knees I spread.

I give in to you.

Naked hand on the thigh.

I no longer can remember my body.

The other holds the whip. You will listen to my voice today.

My father could not speak in my bed, this I remember. Night after night, my deaf and dumb father cracking open my forehead. Burning into my bones. His elbows in my flesh. Fists everywhere. Purple morning skin. My wrists, twisted behind my back, small in the traps of my father's hands. Burning Indian. Blemishes of a father's hurried love. Promises made, spoken in spit. Every inch of him on top of my skin and bones. Him. My father weighed 183 pounds. This, my body will never forget. Sometimes he weighed more. Sometimes less. His knees slightly below my knees. His chin down on the top of my forehead. For years I practiced breathing into his neck. His sweat on me. One day my father died. But that, his death, comes years later. Or maybe it was yesterday. I make marks on the wall. Counting something. Days. Nights. Both. Or desires.

Words are missing here. Sewn beneath the hems of dresses. *She wanted to escape truth and avoid guilt.* At the origin, we stutter. She says something but is not heard.

Desert Father

I count each line of memory cut into my wrists. The red, round sores underneath my tongue. Those tiny pinholes behind my knees. The ones I could not really see. Not with my eyes, only touch with my fingers. This scarred purple skin of my ankles. Rashes without origins. Scratch and scratch until I come. To the bone. Years of taking it. Of opening. I count as if I am going somewhere. The way my father once went somewhere. Traveled into the dark. Left my mother for the desert and a rumor. My father went into that desert and never came back. Not even for one final kiss. Drove the Chevy Impala as far as it would go. Far away from memories of sons and daughters until he found an uninhabited roadside motel. One with no name. A hollow horse. Vacancy. Neon gods in the sky. Lucy sits beneath an apple tree waiting. Some lost memory drowned by the practice of solitude. No sign. This place where music went unheard. Just a disenchanted broom and a Coca Cola machine. One penny, completely alone, in the parking lot. Face up. Once he sent us a postcard. "Sorry had to leave in a rush. I needed to drive a truckload of virgins into the desert. We played harmonicas the whole way to protect us from the mountain lions and the coyotes." He had left, he said, the Impala at the state line.

Then four or five years after going into the desert he died. Leukemia. Cirrhosis of the liver. An irregular heartbeat that exploded in the sun. Pure and simple, he only left behind an abandoned cardboard box. One filled with ragged clothes. Johnny Carson suits bought at Sears. Too much polyester. Frightened moths. Stories of my father's children written in the hands of strangers. Disenchanted dreams. Fables of aggression. Tales of childhood love and loss. The day I dropped that bush-league flyball in right field. My father's world nearly ended that day. He didn't speak to me for weeks. Just looked at me. Shook his head. The image of that ball in his eyes. Utter disappointment. Useless son, put on this earth by a ruthless God to torment him until the end of time.

No one wrote an obituary for my father. Some man called from the hotel. Some man said something about a dead body. Some man said this dead body claimed to be my father. Heritage. A beautiful loser with soft skin. In the evenings your father would caress mosquitoes. Only man I've known who could do that. There are rumors that he deflowered a flea. His touch was that delicate. When the night turned cold, your father could read the accents of people by seeing their breaths. He was a hard worker, your father, and made all of the guests at the hotel smile. Made them feel like they were home. Home. What else is there ever to say to the survivors? My mother wanted nothing to do with the whole affair, the death, the box that protects memory.

Once upon a time, while lost in a locked closet, I wrote on a piece of paper that to this very day I still keep taped to the wall of my bedroom: *December 31, 1988, Tucson, Arizona, a man explodes in some damn café*. A reminder. Dead memory. Heat. Many years later, Lidia wrote to me from San Diego: "Remember Doug that some people go the desert to live. I want you to live. Drive to the ocean. Feel the salt in the water. Taste the saltwater on a woman's body. Do this. Commit this to your skin. Remember."

The doctor had told my father not to drink so much coffee. The caffeine made his body unpredictable. Refined sugars, he warned, just might send him over the edge. Give him serious visions of grandeur. The delusions of a God fallen on hard times. Be careful. And all this mixed with the beer; well, only God Himself knows what might eventually happen. The doctor told him he had a hole in his heart. I could drive a truck through that murmur. Get me some asphalt and fill it in. The doctor had a sense of humor. The doctor is still alive from what I hear. Smoking cigarettes and coughing. He needs love warm and tender.

My father's last lover put her hand on his wrist and said, "I can't tell you how to feel."

The people who knew my father said that he'd do anything for love. Said he was hopeless with just the right touch of self-deprecating humor. He dug holes in sand. Dreamt of China. Slept with coyotes. Shed a torrent of tears that no one ever quite understood. Knelt in the wrong direction. Praised Buddha with the fervor of a born-again Christian. Handed roses to people in airports for no apparent reason. A confused man with clumsy stories. He ate spinach on rainy days. Stared at soap-on-a-rope as if it held mystical powers of invention. Touched a woman, woman after woman, down there. Past that place where God does not allow you to talk. Below, in the place where I can no longer speak. My mouth. Something stuck in between my teeth. A woman peeled skin from her fingers. Raw girl. Her skin. Callused desires. Thumb. I fed on this skin she gave to me. Stoned woman with a broken wrist. Prayed. Fed on small pieces of her desire to devour my touch. Fed on the tiny scraps of paper that she sent to me. Little ziplock bags filled with words that she had pulled off her skin. Words that had made her desperate late in the night. Words that never seemed real. Words that were always separated by concrete misunderstanding. *I can't breathe, she once wrote to me.* Or at least one of the reincarnations of the words in the bag suggested this possibility. *I need water to breathe. Your skin and water. In the water with me.*

I know how to suffer and to beg. Her voice stranded on my answering machine. Never home. *Why are you never home?*

Can you remain quiet? We were in bed. It was a cold spring morning, outside of Pittsburgh. She had to leave. To drive for miles.

I scrubbed her skin with my hands.

Can you sit still? I want you to listen to this song. She put a CD into the car's stereo. I have been trying to forget this song for years now. This gas station. Each time I drive past the Texaco station, I begin telling this story, but stop in mid-sentence. Feel presence. The presence without body.

If only my body responded to these places that she opened. And she said, harder. I remember her voice before she had words. Go down into the muscle and break me open there. My muscles become sore from working her skin back into the earth.

And yet God to this day knows nothing of his son's longing. For thirty-three days. Nights. For thirty-three years. He went into the desert. There, a woman waits. She has never been kissed. Her fingers become rose petals. I remember the touch of her skin in my blood. Ruby girl in the dark wanting to speak words that crack open her throat. That make her into bleeding. She lingers. Her mouth. Her lips parted. Separated at birth, by birth. She wanted to know the kind of speech that startles birds. She leaves her skin on thorns and she cries. Grows terrified of the branches that sleep within her. In the distance, something—a house, a longing for his touch—falls from the sky.

I have never seen my father's dead body. Have never been a witness to his corpse. With these eyes. Ashes to ashes. Have always only thought my father a rumor, some late night accusation uttered beneath dark breathing and impossible fists. *Your father wanted nothing to do with me. Just to use my body. He came home with all kinds of ideas. He wanted me. He wanted.* The body, of this my father, scattered, thrown into the dry winds. Now and then in the dark night becoming day, I imagine him. This father moving inside me. Awkward old man holding himself up against the wall. Bones into the plaster. Midway down the hall and he has to stop to try to find his next breath. His shoulder pressed against the wall. Against the screaming voices of dead saints. One night and then another night and other nights and night after night and he just wanted to find ways to silence me. To stop my body becoming speech, to quit my body, to send my mouth into the quiet.

I needed. Wanted. This return of my body to the place where desire has no voice.

A Cancer Of Desire

Now when I walk through the narrow streets of Sacramento, I speak against this, my body. Flesh and blood. Hungry. Try with these clothes to speak of the desires that others have threatened to nail me to the cross for possessing. To crucify me to justify their love. Dirty knees are the sign of an innocent girl. Chasing my own body down empty alleys. Through paths in the forest. Down vein after vein of blood and the sweet traffic of heroin. Sins against nature. I tap and pinch veins. Seeking to breathe with God. I stroll past little boys standing on street corners. Cars passing. Boys looking and wanting. Boys frightened by their own bodies. Alone dreaming terrified images. They fear that I will crawl into the front seat for them. Wanting not to see me. My own lips hid beneath shadows. Watchman, what of the night. Silent and still. I move my tongue over her sins. To breathe the salt of her desires into me. Swollen ankles tied to the corner of the bed.

I beg.

I pray.

I swallow.

The anonymous skin of unknown men filthy beneath bloody sheets. My flesh carries the marks of God. Lesions. Restless nights on the streets, in alleys, in public bathrooms. Deserted parks by the river. We meet at picnic tables. Not saying a single word, we nod and head over the hill to the horse trail.

I will kill you, the one man tells me. As if I have never heard that one before. As if I should fear him. He is inside me already. My face is pressed against some concrete wall or the rough bark of a tree. It is all the same. A ridiculous cliché of romance, of desire. He thinks he is touching me. Working my body in innovative ways. But he is little more than another Hallmark greeting card from the Land of Oz. I am bleeding. But blood is never death. There is no real pain in any of this. Not in his belt against my back. Not in his cock. Not in his hands. Only a deeper awareness of where my skin stops existing. The place where my skin becomes air.

I live in this world without end. Sit and wait in a dirty booth for another nameless body. Men drifting through their lives with cold eyes. Wasted skins. Empty thoughts. I went through it myself and I won't soon forget it. Every night I dream of immortality. Kleenexes on the floor. The steady stream of a blinking blue light. Images I can barely recognize. Taps on the wall. He shows me what he wants but says nothing. The signs of excitement. Of breaking desires. The vast articulation that can justify you.

I live in this city where fucking is more dangerous than smoking a cigarette. Derek will die. Robert will die. Jamie will die. Is dead. David dies. I open my body. Again. The idea of a body, of my body, was suffocated in me. The fatigue of my bones. Of my mouth. Spit. Knights in armor. In this place I find the happiness of a world without God. Here God suffers the impossible. Confuses his hands with those of the natives. He becomes disoriented, frightened by no shadows. No sun. Here God refuses to enter these hallways. Stands in the entryway. It is too dark even for God. His feet lose their way. And man after man with no name. Thinking if they are dead. Dying. I wipe my chin. Tonight I am weary of the carnival. Tired of polyester. Of zippers. Of lies. Of wanting to tell one story that is not afraid of truth. Of remaining so silent that even I have forgotten that I have ever had a name.

You're no longer there, but nothing leaves you.

Viral Portraits Of Desire
Without Memory

Mystified drunks, wearing shoes that barely exist, shuffle along the sidewalk outside the Garden Exotic Theater. Occasionally they look up away from the pavement at the busted marquee, not out of any spiritual longing to see God but merely because their eyes happen to be pulled in that direction. Their souls have nothing to do with their eyes turning away from the pavement. Other times, when they are too tired to lift their gaze all the way up to the on-again-off-again, flickering light bulbs of the marquee, they look into the eyes of the man made of grease and mud. The man stuck in the ticket booth. Stuck and counting his fingers over and over. Day after day, he carefully counts each individual finger of his small hands before moving onto the next finger. When he has finished counting, afraid that something has gone horribly wrong, he immediately goes back and begins recounting his fingers. One finger at a time. Only two or three fingers are left on each hand. He had lost one finger in some war. Another was lost in the parking lot of a mall. He believes that another one or maybe two were stolen by his ex-wife. One other finger is simply missing, unaccounted for, as if it was never there to begin with. The very thought of losing any more fingers terrifies him. Not for anything in the world does he want to lose another finger. The homeless men of the pavement stop and stare at the slow perfection of this man's marvelous counting. Buried beneath layer upon layer of city dirt, gray ashes, these men chew on cigarette butts in their nearly toothless mouths, while trying with all their might to recall the days when they themselves had inhabited bodies of their very own. Nearly blind from walking beneath the sun for too many years, they rummage among the reflections in the dusty windows searching for some stray idea of their lost flesh. Nothing. Not there. Although sometimes they do discover a hand floating in the air close to their face. Believing that it just might be their own hand, a small part of their body, they open their mouths hoping to taste, to bite into the skin. Drink the blood.

I have been stopped on my way into the theater by these men trapped, in their mystical states, wanting to know if I, too, could see their hands. If I, too, had faith in their hands. I never speak to these men wandering the streets. Although I have kissed many of these men, put my soft lips on their sandpaper lips, slipped my tongue into their desert mouths, have tasted their majestic saliva, I do not think it is such a good idea to lead them on with the false promises of indiscrete words spilled all over the street.

Down the block, on the corner of East and Sixteenth Streets, fat women in wornout, dead-faded, phosphorescent yellow or brilliant orange tube tops stand in the night, wishing upon falling stars and struggling to make eye contact with each passing car. Their rolls of pale flesh fall down off their bodies onto the street. They scratch their skin, claw at the bright red splotches. Body turned inside out. Signs of forgotten encounters with men so ugly that their mothers refuse to remember the names that they had given them so many years ago. These women in their boiled skin remember nothing. Connect nothing with nothing. Think, once upon a time, they might have had a different name and maybe someone had in the far away and long ago pushed them on a swing. Thin women made of twigs also haunt the corner. All bone and no skin, ravaged souls. Women so invisible that when they suck my cock in the bankrupt and cluttered doorways it only feels like the passing wind and a song.

Outside the Apache Lounge, men in t-shirts sit dead in their heavy flesh on concrete stoops and lawn chairs. They never budge. Not a muscle. Years ago when they first sat down here, they were waiting. Dreaming of the steel mills returning with their orange flames and smoke too white for words, of Maz's homer in the bottom of the ninth, of throwing rocks at company men, of Duke Beer in thick bottles (none of that pansy-ass, twist-off bottlecap shit). Now they only sit. It's what they do. When they feel up to it, they look at the girls or they wipe their runny noses with the back of their forearm. All of them have forgotten that they used to be able to talk. They clear their throats, some of them even go so far as to actually open their mouths, but no word. None. They all have heard rumors about their wives sitting at home, talking on the phone, standing on balconies shouting across the alleyway at the kids. But none of these men can find their way back home. It won't matter anyway. The streets are all different now. Some no longer even exist. Their houses crumbled. Most of their wives have left. A few have moved as far away as Youngstown. One drove all the way to Alaska. Some say she will not stop driving until she drives off the face of the earth. Other wives can't even remember how to get dressed in the morning, let alone believe that some husband once lived with them in their wooden houses.

Inside the Apache are the exact same men, except it is too dark to see them. A few women, or at least what appears to be women, sit with these shadow men at the bar. They balance their slight bodies and bones on the bar stools. Retired gymnasts still able to twist and shout. Distorted bodies. Some women already at work. Same old tired mouths and knees. Picking up where they had left off last night. Fists clutching five-dollar bills. Steadying their brittle bodies by holding onto this or that man's knees. There are times when they forget whether they are smoking a cigarette or sucking a cock. At such moments, they smile to themselves, shake their heads, and remember that they haven't had a memory since high school. On slow nights these women sit in the back booth making up tales of their own past. Nothing too extravagant. Some nights they talk and talk until they believe their stories about watching *To Kill A Mockingbird* when they were in high school. They tell stories of how Hamlet tried to give some young blond girl in the film more self-esteem so she would be courageous enough to marry her star-crossed lover and return to Ohio. And when these women speak of Ohio, their voices come alive. One of these women had actually been to Geneva-on-the-Lake, Ohio, had driven all the way on backroads, never once taking the interstate, and it was so much more beautiful than Lake Erie. And she would know because she had stayed in a cottage there for two whole nights.

To this very day, the Apache is still thought to be the darkest place in all of Pittsburgh. God's light abandoned the Apache Lounge over twenty years ago, and the owner has never really been able to find the light switch. The men's room does, at least according to local legend, have a light hanging from a thin chain, a dull 40-watt-bulb. Just enough light to keep you honest. Enough light to frighten men of tangled desires back out onto the streets or into the Garden.

Outside, in the blind light of heaven, these vague souls join the bony men, the ones too emaciated to exist much longer. Men who have fought God, thinking, at one time in their lives, that God had trapped them in the wrong body. These men of bone balance what remains of their desires on narrow curbs, tiptoeing along East Street. Violet bodies throbbing in the crosswalk. Back and forth. Cracked hips and broken heels. Elegant scarves tied tight around their throats. Men forced to hide their thick wrists behind their backs. Men with breast implants that no longer make any kind of sense. I have fucked these men in vacant buildings. Fed on their smells. Teased them with my cock. Asked each of them if they had sisters. If anything, anything at all, about them was real or even close. There have been nights when two, three, four, five, six, seven, eight, nine ... as if I know how to count ... of these men have come with me through the muddy alley into the vacant building. Those nights, I saw God. Relentlessly, I visited God. Each man, boy, girl remaking God in images that I had never seen before. Men step out of the mirrors hanging down from the ceiling, breaking glass, cutting my tiny Alice body. Their flesh mixing with the blood of my body. Bodies so fluid that even I do not know which way I am speaking. My tongue fucked to kingdom come. Shattered beer bottles. Crushed cans. And sharp bones.

Inside the Garden, summer heat fuels bodies with blood. Dehydrated lips and wet tongues. Eyes burned by sweat. Their glances travel off to the side. Elbows nudging elbows. Silent speech. No eyes. Bodies creep closer to each other. Men move up and down the aisle searching for mouths. Pants unzipped. Cocks waiting. Testing the currents of desire. Unseen communions. Faces buried deep in the crotches of married men staring at the images on the screen. Men nervously looking at their watches, doing all they can to ignore my mouth on their cock. They're not one of us. They sit or stand, careful not to touch us, not to even come close to brushing against our jackets. Every once in a while, though, one of them will lock his hands behind my head and slam my face rock hard into his crotch. Remind me who is in control. They push me away when they are done. All in a rush to forget, to return to one lie after another. In this building there have never been any names, only breathing and the mental emptiness of bodies submitting to bodies. I have never before in my life known a world of so few words.

In the Helen Keller Room of The Garden, all is dark. No shadows. No ghosts. Unknown hands, cocks, mouths, anuses. On rare occasions a woman's breasts, her cunt. But that was very rare and such a woman was usually tortured by men refusing to go near her. She became a blind spectator. Just another wall. A tourist looking for a thrill. Women who have always in their sweetest dreams wanted to see men wanting men. Wanting. Usually such women come into the room with their husbands. Pathetic men desperately trying to remain poised. Men who only want to watch their wives watching. Men who are always uncertain about what to do with their hands. Men who are afraid to look. Seeing nothing but their own absence. I touched one of these men once, grabbed, hard, his balls and cock through his jeans. He nearly turned inside out with fear, with joy, with my strong hand fumbling. I put my mouth close to his face so he could smell this desire. Know the desires of my mouth.

I spend hour after hour in this room. Live in this room the way only an orphan can. Hunched over. Hands on my knees, legs spread apart, mouth open. Wet. A man in front, sometimes two or three, one behind me. Others waiting. Difficult to count in the dark. I taste each and every man–their metal skin, sawdust cum, coffee mouth. The saliva of derelicts knocking about in the darkness. Hallways, dark corridors of tongues and fingers. Chaos of flames. Bodies split. The slow burn of a cock nudging, fighting to enter me. Childhood prayers to God have been crushed into these demented walls. Relentlessly shoving. My face pressed against the bricks, against the carpeting on the wall. My face raw from a long day of losing count of the men. We come here one by one, one after the other, for a place to be dead. Here we walk among our own dying. Each fuck more surprising, more deadly than the last. Every last one of us smokes cigarettes. Warm mouths unafraid of cancer. I suck each unloved body with my tender mouth. Suck until time collapses. Each time I swallow, each time another man cuts my skin, I taste a little more of the beauty and of the weariness of Jesus walking alone in the desert. I stand for weeks, addicted, in the center of this burning circle. Here, inside the terror of having nothing to think about, I come to life.

Sacrificial Mutilation

The voices are everywhere. I hear them. Everyday. Behind me in the cafeteria line, inside the chalkboard, inside the smell of Sister Gloria. Standing outside in the cold spring air waiting for one of the nuns to ring the morning bell, waiting for Jesus to die for our sins. Sitting in spelling class. Rocking on the seat. Curled tight into a tiny ball of flesh. *Sit still, Douglas.* But my body just moving. Back and forth. Until Sister Renee cracks my hand. My fragile knuckles. They tell me stories of being a girl and of falling down hills. Of disappearing into the water. They tell me, when I step into the water, that the pull down is an ecstatic movement into forgetfulness. To drown in the fire that burns. To fall into the hole.

I remember Teresa in the room where the blind gather. The surprise of her knuckles, big-fisted muscle girl inside me and some lonely vagrant leaning against an invisible wall, off in the corner dying. All the blessed servants of God whispering. Whips of their own desire against my skin. I can see some of their words in the air. Those words, the ones I can actually see, frighten me.

In the boy's bathroom my body nearly invisible in the mirrors. Gone blind with noise and desire. I try to force my sex into becoming counterfeit to this body becoming, so that the voices will stop, so that she will leave me before I see her. I never expected to touch her. Inside out. Skin outside my skin becoming my lips. Away from this broken reflection that refuses to return. To find my way back into the place where there is rest. But years later, even without the grace of light, I do see her. Here. This. I hear her caressing voice. She drowns the other voices. I travel 3,000 miles across dirt and concrete. Take my body away from the stone architecture of the East coast and carry this blood into the deep blue of the West. The ocean. The sky. A world of color that I cannot understand. A place so fluid that I can barely breathe. I reach toward her body but she disappears in the night. One early evening in Sacramento, we smelled the grass becoming wet. We stood still and collapsed. Once. A fairytale she had told me, whispered into my beliefs. A tiny break in the fabric. Waited to remember to breathe. Just one more breath. A voice trailing off on some phone line. Among discarded words something was born. In the mirror this love.

I can't do this. I can't live inside this pull. Coming toward you. Wanting. My body takes over. Offer this in the body becoming a word.

Unfettered words come to me from her desire. Speech and memory lost. The distant blood and wounds of what we saw when we looked into each other's mouths. Disembodied voices haunted a grief for girlish things. Tiny shoes tacked on a board, holding letters, photographs. Everything falling to the river. Becoming mud and returning to some other place. Drowns.

This body, paranoid, confuses me. Manipulated by a touch.

In the mirrors, these voices return. I hear their words. They want me. Sight unseen. Words that God made. Don Quixote pulls Little Red Riding Hood off the filthy path. Taking a stroll into becoming with sweet girls. They wait for me in the forest, ducking behind bushes around the corner from the school. These words. Word after word. I'm going to get you, my pretty, and your little dog, too. That shrill laughter. My throat exposed to April rains. I want to be the wolf. I want to be Red Riding Hood. Dress in her blood without shame. I want to stand on the corner of Smithfield Street and the Boulevard of the Allies. I want to surprise my father with what I have become. Catch him off guard.

With my fists I break all these mirrors. Punch at the images that I cannot see. That cannot come to me. The glass that breaks me. My way to come to this girl is through this mirror. Glass on the floor. Cut hands. Speaking. Pieces of glass cut into my skin. These broken words split me. Her words, I thought. Her words, I felt. Her words came to me from inside the places that had never before been torn into. She gave me this, her word. A belief in speaking. This. A false saying. Once she told me she had retrieved words she had written to some other. She had broken into his house and had stolen her words back. As if words could be so easily returned. As if they could simply be brought back home. Home. As if words were not under skin. Here. I have her words here. The debris of broken lips. Spilled saliva. God lifts me to another dream.

I no longer can eat, she once told me, without spitting.

To find again the stone that we had placed in the center of our palms. Making wet our commitment with spit and tiny drops of blood. The tips of our fingers bleeding into each other.

Her language remains, for now, imprinted in my bones. I had placed the matter of my desires, this love, in her. To her, this gift. Not detached words, but matter. We talked and talked and talked. Her other mouths made fluid. All we could say with words. No metaphor, our body. This matter. This one presence in the midst of these losses. Her language swims. No longer a present. No longer of this place. No longer of here. No longer in time. The mouth in movement cannot be trusted. Ever. Cannot be redeemed. Cannot become forgiven except in the deceit of forgetting. This giving, this getting. It is why I will never believe Dante and that little girl going into the light. Language can never become a moment of pure light that reaches silence. Language can only be the moment before time begins. The place in the body that is water. It is why, in Los Angeles, there could only be ribs. There. Here. Between us this separation of flesh. A tongue through our skin to our ribs and the mess of tears.

Then she dropped her eyes away from my skin. Here,

inside this here, this is how beauty dies. Her hand unmerciful. Thoughtless. Then the monsters change shape. My tongue stuck still between her lips. She turned her body into a distant voice.

Flying through the air, words gone crazy with mirrors.

In some distance, boys and girls giggle. Thrusting their words in front of me, I see their pointed fingers and my hunger. In the corner of the hallway, I wipe my runny nose with the back of my sleeve. My ridiculous wrists. I wonder what their words want.

Faggot.

Someone in all their glory called me faggot and I blushed. Excited.

Word to word.

This mouth opens. I do not want to be cured. They cannot see. This body moving toward her body. Beast of burden rising in my lungs. Three of them push me down the concrete steps into the spit pit. Their laughter reaching for God. Words fall down on me. My knees on concrete.

***

Dad wanted nothing to do with his voices either, the visions, the barefooted travels into the sand. He also didn't have much of a need for any of our neighbors, especially the ones that knelt relentlessly outside the screen door of our kitchen, chanting odd phrases they had culled from the daily newspapers. Phrases, fragments that they claimed had spoken directly to them of his coming. The coming of Dad.

"I told him," mom said, "I told him three, four times. Time and time again. I told him over and over. He's destroyed this family. People come from everywhere just to see him. To gawk at him. He's an attraction. I'll admit as much, but God says, 'Breathe carefully, desire not too much out of the ordinary, and pay attention to your words.' I told him don't go running off at the mouth. And there he is now. Not a man, but an infant

Jesus. A stoned and cold dragon with philosophy running away from his mouth. Living with coyotes. Sleeping with whatever woman moves his way. Eating raw fish with dragons beneath the seas in some cave. Acting like he is Jean Paul Sartre."

But all my father really wanted from his life was a more reliable television set. One that he could have absolute faith in. A television set for his soul. Not the mutilated one that he thought he had accidentally murdered before heading into the desert. There have been neighborhood rumors of a brick and some sort of hallucination. My father took aim and then an explosion. Some whispers about men in white coats coming to take him away and away. But he disappeared before they could find him.

Now my father is condemned to watching this same deranged, crippled television set over and over again in the family room deep down in the concrete basement. A small twelve-inch screen. Gray, not even black and white. A practically invisible television set that wobbled on the wire stand inside a room desperately waiting to be paneled. A television that flickered, that insisted on skipping a frame every half-minute or so. Hot plastic. My father's blinking eyes. My father trying with all his might to look into the television set to see the reality of his dreams. Ultimately, my dad wanted to spend more time watching television than breathing. To become one with the television set and eventually ascend to heaven with a television set. Rabbit ears and all.

Dad needed his television for staying in touch. "No sense in not knowing where you are," he always said as he settled down into the couch. "It knows all of the secrets that God hides, and it reveals them." My dad wanted to be part of the program. To be programmed. "Whisper," he begged the green glowing tube, "the secrets of the universe to me." He needed it to keep an eye on Johnny Carson and he needed one for remembering the Dean Martin Show and those magical Gold-Diggers. My dad believed in those Gold-Diggers. He was devoted to their every movement. He believed in the backs of their knees, the spaces between their toes, even though they were very seldom ever shown on live television.

My father opened another beer, wiped the back of his hand across his lips. Humid heat of August in Pittsburgh. I could always tell what time of day it was by the way that my father opened his cans of beer. He was the perfect stylist. To this very day I still hear my father opening cans of beer. Every single can opened differently depending on the sun and the moon. My father was at one with Mother Nature whenever he drank. He could feel the pull of the tides. He knew something of their dark desires. And he only drank Iron City beer. The beer of the Golden Triangle. None of that Pabst Blue Ribbon bullshit. And never, not even once, any of that Schmidt's beer. The beer of brotherly love. Brotherly love is simply not the issue when you are drinking beer. Beer is the issue. The day that they came out with Light beer my father nearly died. He thought of abandoning beer as his way of life. His way to his just deserts. He felt betrayed by the modern world of advertising. He even took the problem up with Frank, the barman at The Fox Trot Inn, but to no avail. All the wrong kinds of people were drinking beer in America any more.

"Fuck those skinny wimps playing volleyball on top of the Rocky Mountains. Artificial tans harvested at those unnatural tanning saloons. And I mean saloons, not salons. Drunk on the lack of the right rays. They don't know nothing. Them and that cholesterol, like butter is bad for you or something. I *can* believe it's not butter, not even close. I believe in loads of ideas." Dad was off and running. Him and his mad ideas all amuck.

One day after some uncountable number of beers, he thought about using the magic of speech. Outside, the world was watching. Waiting. Ticking. The neighbors lingered. While sitting on the picnic table in the backyard, Dad came very close to speaking that day. It was a Tuesday in the late or mid 1970s. Nothing was on the television. But Dad persisted with his visions and his absolute belief in promised lands. His sorrow at the fall of gods. His desire for a beloved wife. He knew many things, even, at times, went so far as to have ideas of his own. So he drank what he had led himself to believe was his sixth or seventh beer of the night with all the benevolence of a tired saint touching the electric wounds of an innocent boy. He drank that beer slowly the way he had seen other human beings drink beer, as if it might just be the very last beer in that grand continuum; then, he went into the garage and grabbed another one. Dad decided, after all, not to speak. Just to drink another beer. "To drink and think," he'd always say. "Then perhaps, if the timing is right, I will speak."

Dad admired beer the way most fathers admire their children. He always made time in his life to hold each can in the palm of his hand and stare at its simple perfection before popping the top off. He liked these quiet moments thinking about the power and the grace of beer. The demented cans (those with slight flaws of any sort) Dad tossed into a pile to be drunk on a rainy day. But this sort of rejection always had a terrible affect on Dad. Once, a can haunted Dad for seven or eight days. He couldn't sleep. He mumbled. He had horrifying visions of a prehistoric world. A world without beer. A place of dinosaurs and cave women. Jane Fonda, but no beer. He even missed Raquel Welch being interviewed by Carson. The fourth most important moment in television history. The next day everyone at the department store saying, "She wasn't holding a cat." Dad was so distraught that he went so far as to begin eating again. Finally he realized that it was all a horrible mistake. Just a downright stupid error of judgment. He reconsidered every small detail of the can, and, at the end of a few months of deep reflection, he drank that beer. And he drank that beer with love. I think it may have been raining on the day of the drinking of this beer, but that was not the reason for Dad drinking this particular can of beer. Dad hated mistakes of any kind but the rejecting of this perfectly innocent and flawless can of beer shook Dad's confidence to the very core of his being.

Since then, Dad has become even more diligent in his selection process. Every manmade or god-nodding mistake held within its very being the potential for disturbing all the universe, and Dad–in between drinking beer, sleeping with distraught women, and counting his blessings–simply did not have much time to repair a dysfunctional universe. In a more sophisticated Germanic past such deeply felt observations were called a phenomenology of spirit; Dad, however, called such inarticulate, visionary experiences: beer. And the one thing that he knew better and with a deeper certainty than anything else in the knowable world was that there was and still is and ever will be more beer where this one had come from. Beer was simply that resilient.

Now that Dad has returned from the dead, stinking of high romance and rotten hot dogs, his beer drinking has taken on a whole new dimension. He is a mad lover. A speaker of runes. A man infested by black teeth, but possessing impeccable tastes in clothes and house furnishings. Dad could decorate a trailer home then an ornate mansion without missing a beat. He sold sofas just as easily as he sold couches. Dad could make you believe that the plastic, pink flamingo that you had recently planted, stuck dead into your front lawn, provided just the right sort of contrast to pull together the whole look of your yard. That it truly is an aesthetic masterpiece to have the initials of your name carved into the shrubbery in your front yard. The way that our neighbor Frank Knoltee had had done to his shrubs.

(Instead of an "F" for his first initial, he had cut a "J" into the shrub. Frank was not known as the smartest landscaper in Salem. In fact, he still didn't understand that it was only his initials, not his wife's, like she was not even there, but that is a whole other story.)

Dad could even make you believe that those stiff plastic mockery of flowers that Frank Knoltee's cousins brought down from the back country and had stuck in a truck tire were the next best thing to being there. Those flowers that are not flowers at all but are still loved nonetheless by senseless fools. The sort of flowers not caring one lick or another if it rained. The kind of flowers that you have to dust. That Knoltee fellow was always going around saying that, "One lick, not two." He said that to everyone everywhere. Said it like he was onto something. Like he could ever be on to something. Chomping on a cigar like it was a metaphor. Sucking in the thick beast, with a coy smile. Sucked this metaphor of a cigar with an operatic flair. I'd never seen a man suck in such a dainty manner. At work, where he seemed to always feel especially threatened by women or men with minds, a place where he thought his red sweater gave him more than the simplistic power of a tiny man too fat for his own well-being, he insisted that he be called Deano, his chosen name. A pseudonym, unearned and empty. A title. Some sort of empty signifier proving, of all things, that Jean Baudrillard just might be right. At least when it came to understanding the grandiose stupidity of Deano. Dad thought Deano Knoltee was drunk on power, but then Dad thought how could such a weak man drink a beer? Let alone drink enough to get drunk.

Once Dad leapt a couple thousand feet straight up toward heaven when he saw our neighbor's brand new flamingo. "Deano Knoltee, migod Frank," he said as he tried to catch his breath. "I thought for certain it was real." And that Frank, even though he liked to be called by more proper names than simply

Frank, lit up, went all aglow with the innocent pride of an artist who had just convinced us that his painting was so realistic that no matter how closely we looked at it, it still appeared to be like a photograph. My front yard (he insisted that it was a yard, not a lawn), he told my dad, was like an opaque Italian opera without all those pesky peasants in the pit ruining the experience for all the rest of us. The us. Poor Deano remains clueless.

***

My father wants to know if I have any friends at school. He wants to know what they're teaching me. Honor. Obey. Kneel. Count to ten. Use a comma if you need to pause and take a short breath. My father wants to know if they're putting any ideas into my head. Love thy neighbor. I long for the skinny girl whose knees creak when she stands up to go to the bathroom. The bow-legged girl with perfect biceps and a ridiculous laugh that frightened the heavyset nuns. The girl I would write books for when I grew old and lived in Sacramento. Dad tugs at my hair. Tell me when it hurts. And my mouth knowing nothing of the way for the saying of pain. Knotted hair. If you can say this hurts, then it must not truly hurt. Not on the inside. If you can still speak, then the pain is not real. Pain in such a place is only a performance, a scripted desire that will take you nowhere. His fingers tangled and lost. I think this hurts. Dad. But my mouth empty.

Dear sweet Mother over there at the stove waiting for the tea kettle to boil. The water. Waiting. Her hands on the edge of the stove. Tapping fingers. Mother humming away against the noise. *Shine on me sunshine up with me world.* Any second now the water will boil and my mother will save the water from the burning flames. Her flannel robe. *It's a zip-pi-ty-do-dah day.* The bald spot in the back of her head and I can see her skull. And my own hair so thin and so blonde that it is nearly invisible. *And I'm the hap-piest girl in the whole U.S.A.*

My father kisses me with his lips. An open mouth and a smile as he walks out the door. My mother still at the stove.

***

He wants me. He wants me to shut up so he can sleep.

***

I turn the sound off the television set. On the floor I hold my knees tight against my chest. Press my knees so tight into me that I have to concentrate to breathe. Rocking. I stare at the dumb lips on the television screen. Over my head I hear my father's feet moving across the hardwood floor. Dino jumps on Fred. Slobbering mouth.

I can't find my mother anywhere in the house. She has lost herself again. Years ago, after she had been lost for two or three weeks, I found her counting her fingers. Each of her fingers, slowly, as if her life depended on her doing so. She had locked herself in the car. Old Henrietta, a '57 Ford. Sitting in the front seat without a care. She seemed to have forgotten how the doors of the car worked. Baffled Mommie waiting for a burning tree from God. A fallen apple. A slash of red lipstick scarred her check. Blue eyeshadow too close to her forehead. She simply could not understand, could not find her way for getting back out of the car. Her forehead was bleeding and her lips were moving all over her face. She just sat in that car the way that God sits in heaven. Silent and still. Without a thought. The way God ignored Jesus on the cross. Screaming son of God punished by nails and thirst. Mary sat silent at the feet of her dead son. In the blood of her son, Mary promised to ascend toward heaven. Holding a penny between her knees. She rose from the earth. I tapped on the window, waved to my sweet tiny mother. Mom lifted her head a little, nodded, but kept looking straight ahead out the windshield like there was some kind of road there.

When she was much younger, my mother stood on the

corner of Smithfield Street and Fifth Avenue holding an authentic Campbell's Tomato Soup can and selling history for a quarter. Siren songs of brave Ulysses. Her rag and bone breath spewing forth mighty tales of moon landings, Irish uprisings, some coup in Argentina, and musky evenings under the Brady Street Bridge. "The personal," she always said, "is history too." She was there when some space ship exploded in the sky over Florida and she sang Happy Birthday to a president who wanted her in medieval ways. Her lips swollen and infected by some parasite from the Monongahela River. Her lips, she'd tell you if you stood beside her long enough, they didn't belong to her. She had stolen them from an unspeakable whore, a woman crouched under a piano in the House of Tilden. Liberty Avenue in its heyday before becoming the cultural center of Pittsburgh. Now, there's a lipless whore stumbling around the 'burgh who can't earn a nickel even in her wildest dreams.

Today, my mother comes and goes through room after room in the house, turning on television sets and lights. She has no faith in remote controls. She never was one to trust the space in between. In some rooms she claps her hands until the lights go on in other rooms. She talks softly to television sets, coaxing them to turn on. She's been this way since April 6, 1957. That's when Dad came back from the dead. My mother only owned one camera in her life. I am concerned about the sort of pictures that she took. A drawer full of undeveloped film.

***

My father locks me outside. So I can play.

***

"Don't be out there talking to anyone."

I can't talk to anyone. I don't know how to talk to anyone. I start to talk, to use my hands, my mouth, and everything. Imitate the sounds I have heard. Rumors of voices from the open spaces of her womb. There. Alice places my hand. In some future moment near a river in California. "I need to feel the weight of your body on my body," she tells me. An orange glow in the sky. Some kind of sign. Our awkward bodies on gravel. I feel every stone. My hand. She gives me stones to carry. She says my name as if I do not know it. "I want you to hear my body saying your name. Your name coming from my body. This mouth. As if you are hearing it for the very first time." I can't help but to love her. This body on mine. This one moment. Here. Always here. Present. Then she tears away. Drives a red car. In strange palaces I have heard others speak. Birds. Girls. Machines. Radios with all their schizophrenic static. I can speak inside with the static. There I feel I am home inside the bliss of this hopeful static.

I find some dirt in the backyard. I am not sure how it got there. A place for words. My fingers play in the dirt. I look at them. This dirt feels like my mother's skin. My father's sins. I know the smell of his fingers in dirt. Bite down hard into his knuckles. But I know nothing of the blood of fathers. Cannot believe that fathers bleed. Stains of the past.

The voices are here, too. Voices I dare not meet in dreams. Different from the ones at school. Persistent. Up in the trees. Behind the shrubbery. Sometimes I stand perfectly still with my back pressed against the bricks of our house. My cousin tosses road apples at me. He calls me a girl. A sissie. A monster who watches the wrong television shows. "Holy Cow, Batman, how can he say that?#@*?"

***

My father never learned how to read, or how to write. My mother used to read street signs, directions from maps to him. We drove in circles with the joy of my mother lost in some medicated halo. She read all the local newspapers to him. She told him lies about the pennant race. She tried to make him happy by telling him about another win for the Pirates. Ten in a row. The paper says at this rate, they won't ever be stopped. The Pirates were on a crusade to bring the flag back home to Pittsburgh. And that mattered beyond all else. She invented stories. Acted as if she were reading from the Pittsburgh Post Gazette. My father loved listening to these tales. Illiterate man playing in the dirt with the soul of a sensual virgin. A place for his heart to belong. Nocturnal utterance. Sleepwalking. Talking in his sleep of angels.

Like most mystics, my father drove his body to distraction. Paid the rent for inarticulate prostitutes. Painted everything in the house white because he only wanted us to be visible. "Everything else," he said, "is just not there anyway."

(This is definitively unfinished. A Duchampian paradox. An object awaiting a title. Away from completion. A Joycean epiphany without Derridean clarity. So this will go on and on. Talk about no closure. Lacks that break the Nineteenth century desires into tiny pieces. Here to go, as Wise Ol' Bill would have us believe. Who's to say when this ends and this other begins? Tolstoy stopped writing one day. The end. So I am near stopping as this moves toward becoming Twilight of God.

All of this typing is just to say something different from what William Carlos Williams said to his wife in that note about plums. It's not a poem, dumbfucks. It was a note to his wife. Kill New Critics. Put an end to this tyranny. Critics with nothing better to do than please and appease, than get tenure and lie about meaning. As if meaning can exist without matter. Poets down here don't say nothing at all. They just stand back and let it all be. New Critics with their puffed-up shirts, ironed-stiff collars, eating figs and married to dead men who repeat themselves endlessly. New Critics feigning objectivity while puking forth their own demonic plagues of subjectivity that silence difference. Idle students scribbling down truths and waiting for the pudding. Idle students with-

out a thought, without a care. Students without skin, without blood. Waiting to be named professional. Wearing all the right manners. Killing even the hope of ever reading desire in the words of …. But I do go on. Endlessly. Without closure. I stop. But with plenty of desire. I just wanted to say. To be continued.)

A Series of Followings

I tried to describe a certain exercise of thought; but describing it was not yet exercising thought in that way.

—Gilles Deleuze or Claire Parnet, I'm not really sure. It was translated by Hugh Tomlinson and Barbara Habberjam. Anyway. This was said once.

"Are you following me?"

The Following Is Not A Photograph

The photograph is the end. The dead recording of a moment lost forever. A moment that can never be recalled, that is never returned to. A moment that is without speech. The final desolate knowledge that attempts the impossible.

Scattered and broken markers disappear.

Only the photograph is remembered. There are no remains. A dark space that can only project an image of desire. A cryptic glyph.

The following words (a story of sorts, or perhaps more accurately, a story of discipline) were found lost on a piece of scrap paper floating in the breeze. A paper torn and tossed away by an impatient man. *To photograph the present moment, Old Bill says, which contains the past the future.* This photograph can never be the present. A photograph tends to disobey grammar and refuse transition. None of this talk of discipline or of the desire to be punished, however, can come to be known without some doubt.

The words themselves, like the images etched onto the photographs, had, in the long ago and faraway, once been original. Spoken for the very first time. The origin is always hysterical. Beginning all over the place without knowing that it is beginning. There can never be an *a priori* beginning. There can be no "In the beginning." The pressure of her mouth against my mouth. October 1998. To photograph scent. To photograph taste.

I was told by various sources that this series of three discarded photographs are impossible to reproduce. And, now, no one can remember the places where the photographs were taken; nor can anyone remember the people staring into the camera lens. There are rumors of a basement workshop. These photographs, in the end, can only be questioned. The torture of truth bears down on the ghostliness of the blurred images. Phantom images appear here and there in each photograph unmaking the reality of the captured image. Dogwood trees appear out of nowhere. A girl's arm near the branch of a tree is doubled. Her lips are not able to speak. Reproduced desires becoming invisible, unwanted. A woman slips her pale hand inside the blurred fabric of her dress. Near her skin, beneath the watchful eye of her daughter, a mother appears to have forgotten herself. What emerges, then, are the remains of these estranged photographs. Simple words uncovered by an acute and trustworthy mystic haunted by hideous visions and strange illnesses. The original date of these photographs has been lost. One forgotten memory following after another. The photographer to this day has only been identified as an anonymous plagiarist. It is rumored that the photographs had been discovered stuck in the mud alongside Locust Street in Etna some time after Grandma Schmidt had died. Her death coming in the midst of the Nightly News reporting the Viet Nam conflict.

I think I have real difficulty in experiencing pleasure. ... It's not as simple as that to enjoy oneself. ...
Because I think that the kind of pleasure I would
consider as *the* real pleasure would be so deep, so
intense, so overwhelming I couldn't survive it. ... A
pleasure must be incredibly intense. But I think I
am not the only one like that. I am not able to give
myself and others those middle range pleasures that
make up everyday life. Such pleasures are nothing

The Following Is A False Memory[1]

(Dear Reader, please read the following endnotes[2] with care and compassion.)

My[3] life, my body is the cover story, the story that disguises language. Two lips moving against each other twice at once. Lips in the interzone. Telling one story that deforms the lips of this speaking. A mouth gone astray.

Over coffee in the basement of the Cathedral of Learning at the University of Pittsburgh, Colin MacCabe[4] accused me of being the last High Modernist left[5] on this forbidden Postmodern planet. A boy with his clubfoot stuck in his mouth,

---

[1] I doubt this.

[2] What do you mean you don't read endnotes?

[3] I need to call this into question from the outset.

[4] The truth of this telling is questionable. There are other tellings.

[5] Lukacs.

[6] The most important moment in the history of Modernity (not necessarily Modernism, you know the difference and why the difference matters even though it is also important to recognize that any historical moment inside Modernity inevitably affected Modernism) … I lost my thread. The most important moment in Modernity is the one that transformed the word "looking-glass" into the word "mirror." See the difference? Even Walter Benjamin missed this moment. He was too busy being a flaneur, all those strolls past windows without buying anything but a vague image of desire. Even Andreas Huyssen missed this as he moved to becoming a planeur. The looking glass is the key. Go back to Victorian England and look at the looking (in fact, why don't you just gaze at this gaze and survey your own surveillance?) that is going on there and compare that to our modern, excuse me, postmodern way for looking into the mirror. Do this. Why do you think Dracula is not there? Careful, I can almost feel you opting for the easy answer. Why is Dracula really not there? Have you ever seen a mirror that lacks a gaze?

wanting narrative to no end. "A relic," he called me. Modernism's last scream cutting across the wounded galaxy. "You are a crime," MacCabe simulated. "You and your desires to write onto mirrors[6] against the image."[7] You, my friend, are only a migrant ape caught in the gasoline crack of history.[8]

Hear[9] infection begins. Memorex galaxy.[10] Doug Rice is not any sort of High Modernist ruin. A last tape found in the waste land left behind by Krapp.[11] Who knocks at the door when he's not at home?[12] Never not at home anymore. Always a

---

[7] Feel the temptation. I see you chomping at the bit. Or is it that you should fear the temptation. Repress it. Soon it will pass. Lacan is so lonely tonight. (Gossip at the fence has it that "lonely" is a typing error. A Freudian Slip beneath a Lacanian Dress. If it is, then it is certainly a lovely typo.)

[8] It is not exactly clear who originally said these words. (There is a rumor that they were uttered, not spoken.) Joyce? Rice? MacCabe? Burroughs? The meaning of this passage(#) is also not precise. It is as if the polyvocal possible exegetical maneuvers that lurk beneath the surface are teasing you to interpret. As if indeterminacy is valued over closure. At this point the recording machine breaks down.
(#) Actually this is not a passage at all. It is a series of words contained by grammar and is not going anywhere but remaining still.

[9] Do not for a bloody second think of this as a typo. This is intention! Fuck the French. I'm not dead.

[10] As if living in a headphone culture is not bad enough. Taking our SONY Walkman for a walk while talking on our cellphone. To live inside our house of incest, this culture of the interior. One that shelters everyone from the world. We no longer have a third that walks beside us. Or we become the third. Now we also must decide what is original and what is recorded. What is meant and what is simply said. The difference (unDerridean) between Burroughsian cover stories and Pink Floydesque cover stories is very important here. Inside Burroughsian Nova Machines, the lips telling the story move against the story. A rage against the machine, a refusal to obey the catastrophe of seeking truth. Inside Pink Floyd, on the other hand, the lips move but the eye cannot hear the story the lips is telling nor can they see where the story is coming from. If indeed it is coming. (For further enlightenment close your eyes and listen to any of Godard's early films.)

[11] It is just your imagination running away with you. And here you thought it was an allusion. Or was that an allusion? A passing fad? Popular culture? Put your make-up on fix your hair up pretty, and meet me tonight in Atlantic City. C'mon, meet

machine left wanting.[13] Even though Rice has spent most of his life locked, wanting to bleed, inside an Ivory Tower, he, unlike his precursing[14] foreign agents, does not allude to the past so much as he willfully plagiarizes, pirates, the past out of history into hysteria. Rice is that Joycean moment of transcription. Rice is alphabetical Lucia, disturbed, sitting on the floor overhearing Modernism enacted[15] before her very eyes between her father and Sam Beckett.[16]

---

me. Adorno! No. the Frankfurt School is stunned by Eminem.

[12] This one is more challenging. A bit difficult, won't you say? Even convoluted. Go ahead. Leave the text. Prove yourself. Authorize your voice. Go. Get gone. To a library. A nunnery. Anywhere but here. Don't stay here. You're still reading these words aren't you? Damn. You are disciplined.

[13] For the call of the telephone is incessant and unremitting. When you hang up, it does not disappear but goes into remission. (Read word for word onto my answering machine by an anonymous woman from Berkeley before she moves to New York. Just a reminder. Who's quoting whom. That was not a question. Be less certain of grammar and tone.)

[14] This comes before Caliban is taught to curse. Although how such a coming can come prior to a *pre* is beyond me.

[15] Remember: Modernism is enacted; Postmodernism is the simple re-enactment from an/other source not as privileged as we once thought. Talk about your degenerative echoes on the cliffs of Dover Beach. Lasers in the jungle. Clusters of Honey Nut Cheerios. The collapse of the Great Divide.

[16] MacCabe, the father, at this point suggests that Rice repent. Forget the fear inscribed in a handful of rust. Better to burn out, MacCabe tells me. But I am drifting. Accumulating, layer by layer, elsewhere. [Note the spectacular plateaus of schizophrenic meaning embedded in the preceding textual thread.]

[17] Have you noticed this thread? Moments in place of sites. (Read that sentence more slowly. Trust me, you missed it.) Moments in place of sites. I wonder about this. The possibilities are endless? On weekends I count the chickens (two) and laugh to myself.

[18] This just might be a horrifying typo. Not clear in Rice's original hand if this is the "other" or "author". When reached for comment, Rice suggested that he is, at least in

Rice is inside the hermaphroditic moment;[17] he is inside the erotic space desiring the body of the other.[18] Rice is a parasite[19] being interpenetrated both ways at once.[20] The moment Modernism becomes contaminated by the knock[21] on Joyce's door, as he dictates *Finnegans Wake* to Beckett, gives birth to Rice as a possibility.[22] Rice is that loss[23] of purity, a desecra-

---

deed, not a Poststructuralist; rather, Rice laid claim to actual desire. He touched a woman on her lips. (An Irigarian moment if ever there was one, but of course there can never be one in Irigaray, only forever two.)

[19] But Rice is never a paradigm. Just you try it on. See: Foucault being disciplined by Deleuze.

[20] I insist that you think of William Carlos Williams here.

[21] This is one of the most momentous knocks in literary history. A knock, like Maz's homer, heard around the world. (I am fully aware of history. More aware of baseball history than most other histories. So, yes I know that it was not Maz's homer—the shot that was heard around the world—but Thompson's. The fact that I have to tell this to you directly reveals my loss of trust in you as a reader. My lost faith goes into these digressive explanations, if not downright explications. All this work and I have jury duty next week. So, if this is not a historical slip, a lisp gone mad in the narrative construction of truth, then there must be something else at stake here. You must find the proper cite, place for seeing. And it is not so simple as the autobiographical fact that I am from Pittsburgh. A suggestion, begin: with Hayden White, then go to Edward Said. Keep going. Keep replicating.) This knock would never have come into being in *Ulysses*. This knock is the authentic Postmodern moment. Read this: "The perigraphy, that which comes to a text from the outside, from an intertext, a reference, a library. … The quotation is already on the page before I start writing; it is a stain, a spot. The intertext, when the text covers it up, is a blotting paper blurred by the remains of the entire writing, whose blemishes it has erased" (Antoine Compagnon). That, my friend, is not what I mean.

[22] I still haven't found what I'm looking for. Have you? Look again.

[23] Can't one of these endnotes explain something?

[24] *Sacre Bleu!*

[25] At first, this appears critical of Doug Rice. A sort of self-deprecating humor. But you nod your head ever so slowly as you begin capturing the allusion. And now as

tion[24]. There is little doubt that Rice is nothing more than an unethical roadside robber[25] and his writing a distorted ycho.[26] Rice uses language that systematically corrupts writing. The textual bliss, not Rice, disguises a fundamental act of thievery. In the land of Rice's Happy Babel[27], plagiarism becomes original because so many of the references[28] have been distorted beyond recognition while others are so recognizable that they are always already there, *a priori*. Visibility and surveillance. Such a textual strategy, in its very essence, makes graduate students [29] cry because it leaves them with nothing to do, nothing to write, noth-

---

the sun rises, you realize you are ready to enter a Ph.D. program, maybe even become a member of the guild. A card carrier.

[26] You should know better than to look here by now.

[27] I will help out here. This is not an allusion to The Bible or to Breughal (or whoever it was that made that painting. You know the one that I mean.); rather, it is an allusion to MacDonalds. Reflect here for a moment or two. Think harder.

[28] Postmodernist texts are clueless (in the spirit of Alicia Silverstone), yet the industry of English keeps reproducing itself. Tiny thinkers that prove predestination is not simply a theory. Such an industry persists in procreation of the worse sort. Mirror, mirror on the wall who is the fairest of them all?

[29] Phallocentirc motherfuckers followed by the excitement of an exclamation point! Those who desire a mystery. A clue. Even after reading the previous endnote. Still they insist that there is nothing here. Only their own repeated deferrals. Reading Pynchon like he meant it. Page after page after page. After page. Another page. Damn and you still want to know what happened to the rain forests? Reading Pynchon like physics really mattered. Like he wasn't just kidding. Put a lid on it, Tupperware boy. I fell into this burning ring of fire. Outside the streets are on fire. These buzzing drones that read Calvin and Hobbes with the intensity of R.P. Blackmur looking at the beacon of a watchtower along the shore. Some of you may have been made uncomfortable or worse yet become distracted by the use of the word motherfucker in the opening sentence of this endnote. Zounds! That was not my intention at all. Such intentions are always fallacious anyway. You know that. No ambiguity of any type here. I want you to think hard and long about what is involved in being a phallocentric motherfucker and how you are implicated. Such a critical Canadian anatomy. I am very sorry to have had to have even mentioned any of this. (The category "phallocentric motherfucker" [shall I go so far as to say: "phallologocentric

ing to footnote.[30] Just to point and perhaps say: "See." But most sit twiddling their thumbs, anyway. Confused and uncertain of desire. Only capable of waiting for the end of time or for tomorrow when the source will come[31] and stand before them and make it all go away. Claritas.[32] Cutting-edge[33] graduate

---

motherfucker"] is an inclusive, not exclusive category. Even a female graduate student can be a phallologocentric motherfucker, given the proper instruction, not discipline. [In fact, given the proper discipline, a female graduate student should embrace such a possibility and become this kind of fucker and the male graduate students should run and hide. To say nothing of professors and the fear that such a woman possessed should place into them. I'm not talking that contained and domestic fear in the handful of dust kind of fear.] It is important to trace the history of the word *motherfucker* in part to fully understand the use of it. Begin with a study of race and the Viet Nam conflict. Watch *Full Metal Jacket*.)

30

[31] Careful with what you do with this one. Don't sit in the front row on this day.

[32] Joyce misunderstands Aquinas, Aristotle, and Augustine. Or was that Dedalus? Poor Stephen. In some ways, it is true, I remain a Modernist practicing High Irony. I mean, think about this for a moment, a footnote that you hoped would clarify *claritas*. How lazy are you? All those Norton anthologies that stop you from ever reading. (For those of you working on patterns of images and discourse formations, you may want to note that all of Joyce's influences tend to begin with the letter "A" while all of my influences begin with the letter "B". Now there is an idea for a dissertation. An original Dr. Pepper of an idea if ever there was one. C'mon be a Pepper too! Do research into the history of Pirate Baseball in the 1990's and see an interesting correspondence.) I have also been known to trope about. To say nothing of

[33] Ones who forget they are defined by the center. And forget (or need to forget) that the center is a different center on each coast. Much like the rows of alternative music in record stores in shopping malls.

[34] As if they can own such a formalist style of dress. Just the other day, a student entered my office. Her eyes all aglow with knowledge and desire. On a quest for metaphysical enlightenment. This senseless person lifted her eyes to me and said to me, all innocent and coy, that she was using her own words. "Oh," said I, "you own a language? Go ahead," I told her, "say something in your own words." *As if.* (Some of you may be tempted here to think of this as a reference to popular culture and slang. Idiomatic structures. How delusional can you be?)

students, in their[34] proper[35] attire, remain innocent.[36] They speak from inside tombs of nomadic slippage in logocentric discourse, write feminism in patriarchal sentences. God ain't dead. He's in the grammar.[37]

Perhaps the time has come to wander through doors left ajar.[38] Back alleys dealing flesh and manufactured[39] desires.

In the end Rice's textuality[40] is a piously forged misquote. A ventriloquy that is false to its desiring origins.[41] The textual troubles began because Rice had left his signature[42] (one

---

[35] See, I told you so.

[36] Faulkner, p. 28.

[37] Symbolic castration, a just question.

[38] Let us go then you and I and leave behind the old way of speaking over a text and let us begin to work on the threshold. To step into the places of random, seeming barrenness, emptiness, or neglect, and bring back an abundance. To take on this work means to leave the mainstream and the cutting edge behind as mere photocopies of themselves, each other, abandoning the ordinary world of jobs and housing. Leave behind the mythological lies embedded in trying to be professional. Leave behind your yearning to enter into the profession of coffins. Threshold life is (I shall stop myself here.) ... I'm not sleeping.

[39] Originally Rice had misspelled manufactured as manufractured. Talk about you postmodern Freudian slip.

[40] To be complete (especially in the sense of the incomplete fragment, which is always more difficult to imagine, since silence speaks always and only to spite itself against itself) ... To be complete books must contain counterbooks. Such counterbooks must be unspoken, nearly invisible. Leopold Bloom on the beach. "I accept charges of plagiarism, when applied to me, but I do so only in quotation marks as a metaphor, say, but not otherwise." All serious literature, after all, resembles a pond of quotations in which the currents not only visibly replicate themselves, but also sink into the depths and rise up from them again. Such a concept is very important for Rice's theory of resurrection, which is different from his theory of adaptation, or Acker's theory (which is not her theory at all but merely one thrust upon her by unthinking men and women seeking the Holy Grail or some sort of security blanket for a job well done!) of appropriation.

that he adapted, appropriated, from Marcel Duchamp and other unnamed French[43] guys) on the polysemic sutures[44] of words. Sutures that visibly disturb Mary Shelley.[45] Rice is very sorry for having done this.

---

[41] Rice casually lifts the lifewand and the dumb speak. ["These quotation marks are too late."]

[42] After giving a talk at the University of California, Irvine, Derrida told me the check would be in the mail. I asked him who signed it. He said, he and R. Mutt did. Together. A joint venture. The same pen. Have you ever tried to cash such a check? Mutt signing a check for his dentist, Derrida signing any check. What remains a signature?

[43] Derrida. Barthes. Bataille. Blanchot. Kristeva. Cixous. Irigaray. Forgive me for naming the unnameable. What was I thinking? Beckett!

[44] A mark across the forehead. An interruption that results in interpretation. A disease that can only be never owned. A possibility that is no longer possible. An insight that replaces de Manian blindness in a way that settles the score. A different way to masturbate. A dissertation that pleases. (Once upon a time and a very good time it was, a friend called me from somewhere and said: "I am writing($) my dissertation on pleasure. I am using Barthes and his theory of bliss. Can you help me?" I thought for three(#) days before responding. "No. I don't think anyone can help you.")
($) For those of you who do not "see" this as a typo and who do not understand the philosophical necessity of this parenthetical sign that I used to attract your attention, to seduce you to defer my narrative by having you follow this other thread down to here, pray that God forgives. Or read Stephen Pfohl's work or watch Jalal Toufic's *Photocopy Degeneration* video and think more. Think more. Damn you. Same as it ever was.
(#) This is an allegory.

[45] Dear James Whale,
    When such sutures need to be made visible the real becomes that much more invisible. Visibility is a trap. A readily apparent seduction. One that is read far too easily in the comfort zone. One that allows us to feel we are merely being entertained. (Kathy Acker making visible Dario Argento's sadism or his misogyny is altogether an other story. One you—you know who you are without me saying so—cannot possibly know. In the spring of 2001, Doug Rice gave a talk that became a making visible of such shadows, the subtexts of Acker rupturing Argento, only to be greeted by big strong men protecting their women from seeing their lives being assaulted. Finally a woman braved the tide and spoke against such a fairytale that her

male counterparts created. All these men saving their women. Accusing Acker of conduct unbecoming a woman and of Rice perpetuating such ideas. "What are we to do?" she asked. Male expectations of female spectacle. Males designing high heels. Males designing the underwire bra. But I digress. [Granted, I cannot know of any of this, since I am dead. Since, historically this all happens now after my death and we all know here in America that the past is dead, unable to matter or mean or speak. We know in a pragmatic way that Ronald Reagan has been elected president again and again. And if I had just voted one time. Or if I had just lived in Florida where I could have voted any number of times. Fuck history, the toy of men.].)

Your film, Mr. Whale, is nothing more than an Oprah moment! Recall that trauma, medieval trauma, is seen without speech. No one can speak trauma. Trauma simply is. It always already is visible as a mark on the body. That is why, when someone says they had a traumatic experience, the first thing you should ask them is to allow you to see it. Show me the trauma on your skin. If it is not there, it is not trauma. (Much could be and perhaps should be said here about tragedy, as well, but I fear digression.) All those medieval moments in public, the display of sins, were not spectacles. They only become spectacles, create a society of spectacles, at the point when Leopold von Sacher Masoch and the Marquis de Sade are condemned to isolation. To writing. Locked in a room. So now everyone follows a script to create a scene that can only be imagined and includes safe words that eliminate the entire notion of pain. So the bottom begs: "Oh please, please hit me. I've been ever so naughty!" Why doesn't the Top just refuse. Just say no and walk away. Or when the bottom inevitably pleads: "Oh no, no, don't!" Why doesn't the Top just say, "Okay." Isn't that denial more painful? All this narcissistic exhibitionism (too often it is the same in some writers). Look at me. Watch me. See me. Feel me. Heal me. The saints rejected such simplicity. They wanted to be locked away inside walls where there is no control. And even such a Debordian society of the spectacle is now gone, can no longer be since the end of spectacle can only be the creation of cliché. Just as the end of democracy can only be fascism. (That is not necessarily a bold critique of the current presidential regime.) So now we can only live in a society of clichés. Springer, Oprah, Leeza, and on and on, are not spectacles but clichés. Can't you just think a little harder, a little more deeply. A world of real tv. (Sorry, Real World TV.) (My mother bought a videotape of a fire in a fireplace. She puts the videotape into the VCR every Christmas. And our television set becomes a warm and delightful fireplace filled with joy. We sit and watch. One day we will all be dead. But not the tape. [See Atom Egoyan's films for further support of this general argument.] One Christmas, I tried to toast marshmallows in the televised fire. Chestnuts roasting and all that. Talk about being sadly disappointed. Another Christmas, I told my mother, "wouldn't it be interesting if we could be watching a videotape of the destruction of our family, instead of this simple fire that is not real?" I was told to leave the dining room and eat in the kitchen with the other children and their insane ideas. Sitting there, I could hear more clearly the crackling of the logs on the television set.)

Remember, though, that *incest*[46] may be nothing more than an anasemic encrypting of the word insect.

To be crucified by an invisibility of the suture, however, is to become a movement toward power. A suture that is without a being. One that surprises. One that sneaks up on you.

Leave my monstrosity alone. Do not mark the daemon with your signs, with your simplicity. Remember what happened on the wedding night. Everyone in circles. Wagons circled around poor Elizabeth. The daemon was as much her creation as it was Victor's invention. And there is a difference between creation and invention. Fluids. Afterbirth fucking. Everyone looking for the present of body and missing the presence of desire. Until the scream becomes the body coming to trauma. And she is penetrated by a song that carries her to the tundra, that she cannot control.

Sincerely,

Mary

[46] He do the policemen in different voices.

The Following is Reading

In the spring of 1979, I was arrested by the thought police in the English Department of Slippery Rock State College. These men actually saw that which was not there. They, with their lackluster humor of a Lacanian sort, discovered my lack of originality. My only aura, a black outfit with a cynical wit, complicated by the precious afterglow of a photocopier. Frequently, I was interrupted and distracted by traditions and the desire for "an" individual talent. A nod, I once overheard, is as good as a wink to a blind prophet.

I am driven by memories that I too often forget to cite.

Like a diseased fugitive I take leave of words. An unpacked library with erased copyright pages. A pirate traveling down a lost highway. Detourned. 57 channels and my remote is broken. Always already on. And on. *A priori.* Born with the television on. Nothing. Silence. I gaze at nothing. The blank screen of the television stares back at me. Wanting me. Have you ever turned on a television set? I have. Following your lipstick traces with my innocent eye.

She would never say where she came from.

"I am a virgin."

"No," she said. "No, you cannot say that."

I read nothing in ways that most people dream of reading Dante. Between the lines, white dust and kaleidoscopes of visions. I pick up words along the way. Pack up my ermines. Step into gutters and steal debris that had at one time appeared useless. Back in 1922 when the tourists invaded Trieste, Paris, London, I stole image after image from men with holes in their pockets. But in the 1970s, while listening to music so bad that I nearly died, I washed my hands of the whole messy affair. I am no plagiarist.

He stood before me with evidence. Full metal jacket. Hard core. A red pen and a shit-eating grin that will come to no good. At least not to any of that good old medieval recycling of shit-into-splendor good. This man with no imagination, just a tape recorder and a highlighter, accused me of conduct unbecoming. His hands blackened by newsprint. Fractions of words rubbed into his skin. Blurred words with no idea. And he knew nothing. Just didn't get it. No, not at all. How I loved making my hands dirty all through childhood. The smell of newly run-off stencils. Me and *silly-putty* wreaking all sorts of havoc on copyright. Rubbing and flattening the *silly-putty* on the comics and lifting it up ever so carefully, like I was making an original readymade. Like I was Duchamp or Warhol.

I tried to explain to the professor that I was no criminal.

I heard myself say, "Style is the only legitimate quotation marks. And style is more challenging than simply typing inverted commas as if that grants credit or authority to an echo from the dead past. And," I continued, "the past is only dead in such coffins. For me the past remains. Alive, she cried, it's alive, infecting me with curses."

He wanted nothing whatsoever to do with me. He was a man without hope.

"Only a reader can plagiarize. You," I told him, "you are the real criminal. It is you that took all my illegitimate, damned references home as if home was the same as it ever was. You took them back to their origins as if that was their destination. I robbed them of such sanctuaries. Made them nomadic. How dare you fuck my sweet innocence."

Many years later, so the story goes, Kathy called me after *Blood of Mugwump* was published. "Doug," Kathy said, "you have stolen three of my words on the very first page of your novel. Word for word, mine."

I told Kathy not to worry, that readers would by instinct take them back to her text. Safe and sound. She was not convinced.

"It will not be the same, though, will I, Doug?"

"No," I replied. "No, my mouth your words. This saliva lost becoming wet."

"And you call this an autobiography. How can my words make your life?"

Nostalgia. A photograph of Kathy and I with our hands pressed down on the glass of a photocopier going about its business. All aglow. Basking in the sweet Benjaminian aura. Nothing but replicas as far as the eye can see. Mirror, mirror invoked as the originary desire of the artist. In the shuffling madness, the distant background, an echo nearly lost, graduate students come and go. Disguised replicants armed with Kodak Instamatic cameras. Tourists mad with clicking. My murderous mirrorhand accuses me, not in so many words, of having stolen original copies of letters never mailed from the Parasite Café.

The Following Is No Longer Poststructuralism

This is my writing utensil. I show her my pencil. My red pen.

'Nuf said. I should stop here. But I must go on. Follow me. Can only go on. Go on without end. The drive to tell secrets. To crack into the mundane world.

The French have no authority to say. All those lovely syllables, lovely letters falling into the gutter. Unspeakable horrors. The prettiest moments in the French language are left unsaid. Tossed aside.

Who is dead, she asked me. None of this is inside quotation marks.

Don't put that into your mouth. Only God knows where it's been. Overheard as a child picks up a wretched and naked candy bar from the sidewalk in Etna. Like Samuel Beckett's Wakean knock, I leave the world in. The wor(l)d creeping in by surprise.

Once upon a time, here the actual story of fictional truth has a beginning. I slept with a real woman staking claim to being an authentic post structuralist in Binghamton, New York, of all places. The experience, I was told, would be even better than the real thing. As we walked across campus, she tripped over a rambunctious root. Of a tree, I think. Fuck me, she said. Floating. I was uncertain of her subjectivity. The signifier free of the signified. I wanted her desire. I tried with all my might to read her, but tired beneath the fecund weight of her multiplicity. A multiplicity that too often turns to simplicity. All those structures lacking connections. Everyone trying to go solo. Her house was littered with texts. Most were nondescript. In her bed we exchanged notes. Heralded each other across the way of our bodies.

She said to me, "I am a post structuralist." Her voice filled the room with what at first glance appeared to be indeterminate meaning.

I felt compelled, forced, to put her in her place, away from the world, into words. "You can't say that. Only I can say you are a Poststructuralist. To say, 'I am' is to say I know not what. Especially when your I am is placed inside the coffins of quotation marks."

She smiled.

"Me Tarzan, you Jane."

She wept. Stuttered and failed to give any utterance to her desires. We tumbled out of language into bed. She wanted me to use protection and practice safe sex. I reminded her that she was—in deed—a post structuralist; therefore, using protection and practicing safe sex is nothing more than the redundant behavior of mocking cynics, radical skeptics afraid of giving birth to tragedy. We burned maps and took wrong turns. In the morning she sat on the edge of the bed, her face in her hands, sobbing.

You see, after all is said and done, you can't really be a poststructuralist. You can only say.

I made her take it all back.

The Following Is Digression

A character in my new novel, *Twilight of God*, exists outside quotation marks and has undertaken the monkish task of rewriting William Faulkner's *The Sound and the Fury* in a nearly medieval macaronic style that riddles Shem the Penman. This character uses the exact same words from Faulkner's novel the exact same number of times that Faulkner had used each word. Reproducing that New-old High Modernist desire for difficulty, this character decides to add one word that is not in Faulkner's original. He does so, thus problematizing the enterprise of reading. A year later, he discovers not only that his narratives is suffering from an infection – a sort of Eliotic embodiment of the affect of an "individual" on "tradition" – but also that his original copy of Faulkner's novel is corrupt. A page is missing. The magical tour-de-force that then follows ecos (*sic*) Calvino. This character is rabid, foaming at the mouth. He only is able to experience life inside the narrative structures of others, keeping his own *I* out of it entirely, while keeping the other eye out for the rube. This character, trapped by the metamorphobic impossibility of speech, is reminiscent of the protean performance of the *indelibile* language inside the Shem episode of Joyce's *Finnegans Wake*. Letters, themselves, are alive. They teeter on the seductive edge of promiscuity. Manner can only be matter in Joyce's *Wake*. Letters are alert to changes. Unlike Gertrude Stein's a rose is a rose is a rose syntactical disorders (or Acker's play with Wittgenstenian repetition [Recall the two warrants {not doubled warrants} that Wittgenstein set forth for understanding a sentence: "the sense in which it can be replaced by another which says the same" and "the sense in which it cannot be replaced by another" {neither of these warrants are meant in any way to replace the other}.]), Shem's letters are disobedient, uncivilized, practically illiterate infants of the night, nearly vampiric in their ability to shift shapes. Watch as *indelibile* becomes *indelible,* with the casual slip of an *i* before your very eyes.

The Following Is A List

The following is a list that has been written by a foreign hand that is no longer identifiable. A collection of epileptic epistles written in the traditional literary form of the epiboly[1] . Some of these epistles are rather blunt (akin to a direct blow to the word hoard by, say, a dirty, infested needle filled with undisciplined desires), and may, at first glance, appear to be aphorisms. Under the circumcisions[2] , however, aphorisms would, in deed, be inappropriate. Wittgenstein and Hendrix collaborating on a soundtrack for the experience of going unto a shopping mall. These epistles have all been forged, neither from the smithy of my soul nor from the sacred fount of my romantic despair but from nowhere, the palace of nomadic bums, a pleasure dome of rice (*sic*).[3]

1. A spot marking an absence.
2. I am mistaken.
3. It is hard to listen to the sounds of a train when you have to stay put. Sit still.
4. The mystic writing pad.
5. In a dream I see the place where the garment gapes.
6. I am writing.
7. Permanently unclear.
8. She lacks an antecedent. Biographers and critics alike have begun tracking this signifier. She appears to be an indirect reference to … well, I am not at liberty to say.
9. Mutilated sentence.
10. Fuck tattoos. Mall-driven consumption of the radical. Unless they come. From the inside. Push their way out. Alien babies that become as recognizable as breathing. *I can't help this.* Everyone who has a tattoo should say, "I didn't want a

tattoo."

11. "Please do not quote me on this. These are not my words."
12. I was born into Tradition, a misbegotten, queer foreigner.
13. Uncertain promises that feel very much like fucking.
14. "To read" means to pick up along the way, to borrow. The way she becomes I while I become she.
15. I is inarticulate.
16. Have you ever put a fist into a poststructuralist? It wakes them up and ruins their theorizing for at least 19 days.
17. At this point it would be helpful to reread *Agamemnon*.
18. Forgotten sources that tempt necrophiliacs to come.
19. This is true: Somewhere in the Midwest there is a strip mall named *Villa Baudrillard*. It is open for interpretation. You never arrive. There are road signs that provide you with suggestive directions and you do desire to come. To arrive. To get there. To experience the experience of the mall. You follow each sign, each direction, each herald, as if they really mean to take you there. In the *Villa Baudrillard*, all that is for sale are the *for sale* signs.
20. Automatic for the People. The Who Sell Out. Victoria's Secret is no longer a secret. We do not live in a society of spectacles and images. We live in a society of cliches.
21. "Sign, sign, everywhere a sign, blocking out the scenery, breaking my mind."
22. Last night I dreamt that you and I had words.
23. I now dream I want to be stained.

---

[1] This form requires a footnote.
[2] For a moment, you stop thinking and think this must be a typo.
[3] Get to work you giddy and resourceful wonderboys and girls. The allusions in this sentence alone are overwhelming, breathtaking.

The Following Is Somewhat True

I misbehave in the space where the stripper's garment is made to gape. I misbehave as a well-intentioned confusion. Messy boy with no sense of syntax. Words strewn all over the place. Bloodied remains of an undisciplined grammar. Punish. I want.

In fifth grade, I pass a note to Joanne Brungo. Her father is a dentist. For some reason this matters. It is a simple note: Why do you get to be a girl? (Today I would get tenure for posing such a gender conundrum that calls into question the notion of choice, of the binary, of *all that is solid melts away*.) Back then, I was reported to the nuns for some sort of civil disobedience. My parents are called. Monsignor Henninger tells me to be quiet. He tells me that I was made in God's image. Like it or not.

I think of Joanne. When we arrive home, in front of the rest of the family, my mother washes my mouth out with soap. I try to tell her to leave my mouth out of it. My mouth has nothing to do with it. She is screaming for me to watch what I say. If I'm not careful, she tells me, it might all come true.

I fall in love with using words. I say: Joanne Brungo. But nothing happens. Like the Wonderbra, the Miracle Bra, and Maidenform, the placing of Joanne Brungo into speech simply does not work.

I become a poststructuralist without knowing it.

The Following Is Hallucination

Theseus' ship is falling apart, decaying dead wood. As the ship sits in dry dock, rotting, Theseus' men replace each rotten plank. The ship remains the same ship, even as some of these old planks are replaced by new ones. The men store the rotted wood in an old warehouse. After many years, the last of the original planks is removed from the ship and replaced by a new plank. Now there is enough old wood in the warehouse to rebuild the ship. The men do so.

Two ships now float on the waters, side by side. Which one is the original ship of Theseus?

In a world – social as well as aesthetic – of anti-oedipal cover stories echoed in minor languages, Shem-like pelegariasts abound. In 1990, I was escorted out of the Carnegie Museum of Modern Art in Pittsburgh for taking a photograph of Morimura Yasamusa's "After Faye Dunaway" self-portrait. I was told that I could buy a copy of the exhibition catalogue at the museum store, and that taking photographs of artworks causes the artwork itself to deteriorate. I said, "Yes, that is the point. I want to participate. I want in." Pentimento! The lifting of layer after layer of invisible textuality until the bone is rendered. Re-pent. Made apparent. The naked eye and history converge. My plagiarizing originality is created in layers, with each image track both obscuring and enhancing portions of the previous image. The past emerges, hesitant, visible traces of a layering, with, in, against the present. Presence. Kathy's tongue in my mouth.

The Following Is A Glossary

Anonymous referentiality
Paradoxical authenticity
Self-citation
Master/slave (or flayfutter)
Letter from litter
Litter from letter
Wastebasket
Unsystematic penis
Murderous mirrorhand
Counterfeit photocopies (and seedy ejaculations)
"She plucked my peepee!"
A tergo
Expropriate tongues
Parasitical origin
David Cronenberg meats (*sic,* to be or not to be, can it be?)
Atom Egoyan
Wait just a moment
Wait a just moment
What is going on here?
No one can steal my words
The eloquence of the vulgar
Raiding coffins
Window shopping
A pile of dirty rags
Sexual penetration and the hymen collide

Born to Ruin:[1]
Bloody Fragments Uprooted Violently From The Pages Of An Abandoned Introduction To Doug Rice's Skin Prayer

By: Larry McCaffery

He went down to the desert city where the rattlesnakes play
And left his dead skin by the roadside in the noon of day.

There was a woman he'd met in a desert song
A little while later a song came along
Looked at that boy's smile and called it home
And that night as he lay in bed the only voice he heard was his own.
—Bruce Springsteen, "Cali Song"

---

[1] This essay is an essay of remains. A guilty and jilted syntax and a grammatical nightmare. Larry McCaffery wrote this in the language of the desert. Climbing mountains somewhere outside of Borrego Springs and then traveling dusty roads to Mexico and Idaho. To this day the essay remains untranslated, scattered. The very terrain of the desert. Shifting sands that covered punctuation and ate verbs and pronouns. Some of it has been infected by Doug Rice. The run-on sentences are frightening, but the density of McCaffery's private madness demands careful attention. Demands to be reread. In fact, the writing of some of these sentences is nearly a performative response to Rice's "own" gung-ho style. Mccaffery is practically becoming Ricean and the townfolk in San Diego are worried. McCaffery has discovered, but not completely figured out, a connection between Bruce Springsteen and Rice. This connection has a significant impact for understanding all of Rice's work. McCaffery is getting back to that connection, but not here, not now. Some of the connections do, however, surface throughout this essay. If you find them distracting, please feel free to think harder.

I. Guilt-Ridden Prefatory Remarks

"Sister, I won't ask for forgiveness—my sins are all I have."
—Bruce Springsteen, "Dead Man Walking"

Many of these words are stained with the ink-blood that once circulated through the innards of my critical facilities, bringing it nourishment that helped sustain it as a coherent entity, but which now, having been liberated from the prison-house of the body, can only drip incoherently, assembling mysterious patterns in hues of hallucinatory redness on the unviolated whiteness of the blank pages of my abandoned preface, which were recently discovered while drifting aimlessly in the desert, enroute to the oblivion that Rice himself has written about with such hallucinatory power and vividness in *Skin Prayer,* the major new work-in-progress excerpted here. Rice, together with his long-time collaborator and alter ego Bruce Springsteen and numerous other lesser-known voices (*too* numerous, in fact) who have been crowded together inside of Rice's head, has been working on plagiarizing from the wasteland of narrative ruins since leaving the fascist despair of Kent State University, Salem. In *Skin Prayer,* Rice transforms these awful incarnations of an anxiety of influence into flesh-like words spilling over into his throat and mouth with a kind of violently-crazed, ecstatic, religiously-inspired delirium.

II. Lost in the Flood

Yo Doug,
Your new book is fucking incredible. The whole world is out

there. Cover me.
(Words stranded on an answering machine in a hotel room in Santa Carla. Rice had been on the beach and received this message too late. The details of Rice's walk into the ocean are sketchy and need to remain secret.)

I have stumbled upon a few disturbed words concerning the perils of terminology (literary and otherwise) evoked by Rice's *Skin Prayer* with its constant deluge of Apocalyptic Warnings, its deconstructive and reconstructive strategies, its blasphemies and transgressions, and other equally turbulent and unsettling features, any one of which is capable of pushing readers out of the comfortable boats they normally use to navigate through literary texts.

But literary navigators of all levels should be forewarned, for Rice has constructed *Skin Prayer* in such as way as to unsettle even the most self-assured readers. Thus, even those readers who have had no trouble keeping their balance while reading the works of William S. Burroughs, Kathy Acker, Georges Bataille, Pierre Guyotat, and other authors with whom Rice shares affinities may well find that maintaining their equilibrium during their passage through the pages of *Skin Prayer* to be an uphill struggle, an exercise in futility, a journey into chaos. This literary *tour-de-force* results from the radicalism of Rice's formal methods and the sheer visceral intensity of his prose.

One of the most disconcerting features of Rice's prose is the manner in which syntax and grammar are employed. Rice deliberately confounds the way that syntax and grammar operate in daily speech. It is almost *as if* Rice is dyslexic and forgetful. He cuts a six-inch valley in the middle of my skull. Pronouns shift unexpectedly. Rice desires Teresa, Alice. Is becoming Teresa and Alice. Rice steps through his bone into them as they come out of his skin. Rice's tenses (the muscle of his philosophy of history) move through complex uncertainties that befuddle the reader and create an enjambment of time and space; tenses move past the past into the present beyond the past through the present. Rice's language is never in the same place twice. His narrative is a river becoming. Reading Rice is like trying to step into the same river twice. Characters bring rice water. Carriers. Broken chairs of narrative construction are mended only to burst. Descriptions appear out of nowhere forcing readers into uncomfortable moments of space and time. Throughout the narratives I could not remember how I came to be there. Here. The complex work of performing forgetting. Rice always pushes and alludes to *Hiroshima, Mon Amour,* and to the work of Jalal Toufic as a way for speaking the forgotten that is not yet forgotten. The difficulty of forgetting. Brief snippets of narration appear but can only lead elsewhere or to the desert. Or ocean. Beyond water. Rice's desire to move his body language into becoming water. Rice's syntax is longing. A threshold. This shift in geography for Rice. The move toward water, that pull, here for the first time, marks a new passage in Rice's narrative desires.

The effect of Rice's rich style is to force readers to abandon their reliance on structures that give their reading experience a sense of continuity and meaning. A grandiose "fuck you" on the plague of the professionalization of reading (via modern English Departments and Talk Shows, especially a "fuck you" against New Critics and poststructuralists; moreso against the ones who *think* they can *speak* of *not* speaking.) Clearly Rice has been influenced by Jean-Luc Godard's jumpcut editing style and the use of arbitrary noise. Noise that is typically filtered, Rice embraces. ("Larry McCaffery turned me onto Hal Wilner. This is his fault. I also saw John Zorn's music on my wall. And Attali's work. Blame that on McCabe and Simon Frith." Rice in an interview with a Serbian newspaper reporter.) Dante's buzzing bees in the *Inferno*. David Blair's gaze into the heat of the desert. Soft machines that melt. Without the traditional genre-driven structures to provide balance, Rice forces readers to engage his broken textualities, his crippled and inventive syntaxes, in innovative and sophisticated ways that are not typical of traditional reading practices. Get no. Can't get no. Satisfaction. Rice invents (or re-invents) reading. His textuality teaches readers to read.

"Why read," Rice once asked me while standing at a crosswalk in San Diego, "if you already know how to read? Why read if you are not becoming startled? Taken aback? Jameson's reading of Joyce pulling us up by the bootstraps and disciplining our act of moving our eyes over print in a new way. Old Jimmie pushing Aunt Josephine out of her rocking chair."

At a bar in Providence, I overheard Doug Rice and Kathy Acker talking late into the night about reading. Their desires. Hunger for places where word and body become pleasures of the text. Sam Delaney sat silently in the corner with Paul Auster.

"I want to read you."

"And you I."

"You can't write," Rice told Acker, "without recognizing the bodily act of reading. Writing is only, always, reading."

"We write for our own pleasures of reading," Kathy said. She put her hand near her skin. Her lips. Kathy was tired that night. Too tired from jetlag and Rice from a nearly two-day train journey.

"I'm writing here," Rice played with his drink and began scribbling on Kathy's arm, "because reading does not exist any more."

Remember. Daddy was a black sheep. Daddy was a whore. (There is a misquote redirecting blame, guilt, and responsibility. If this doesn't get me on Springer. What has slipped here? Who is misquoting whom? Who is replacing whom? Why? How? Set tehse secrets free from the dusty words lying under the carpet.)

Rice pulls readers into the visceral nature of language. Language is always *here,* never there. Rice does not so much write the language of the body as he returns to the primordial places of language and, from there, Rice breeds and breathes language. Rice's work is a breathing of language. A raiding of the mediaeval word-hoard. Rice shapes those places in all of us that typically we hide beneath layer upon layer of repressed desires. Chaos. Rice has an aesthetic that breaks the codes of this internal chaos. He shapes the secrets. This pain. The houses of language are made flesh by Rice; readers must, therefore, focus all their attention on what is immediately in front of them: on the words, images, sentences which emerge from nothing, from nowhere, and which "go" nowhere. He builds sentences that demand to be read and experienced purely as themselves, as processes of deleuzional becoming in which the past and future become irrelevant. Infected sentences. Inflected bodies. Sentences that are, like Alice through the looking-glass, always growing. Rice pushes into the now. Here. Rice writes over and over, or demands, throughout *Skin Prayer* that bodies come into language in the here. Come to the here. Not as a rejection of becoming but as a place in time for bodies to touch skin.

(I know Rice (w)rote most of this book from inside. From in there. He was there (w)riting his way through to the other side.)

III "I'm A Dead Man Talking" (*from Springsteen's "Dead Man Walking"*)

Since Rice is so intent on throwing down the challenge of being able to recognize the historical identity traits of the literary forms he appropriates, it makes perfect sense to this critic to permit Rice the respect of at least making a provisional effort to identify the genres and sources of his misbegotten desires. Here then is a list of genre categories, literary terms, and classifications, which might be used to describe Rice's work. Inevitably such a Foucauldian paradigmatic method fails to satisfy. Rice's prose style is more like the table of accumulations in Deleuze and the plateaus of becoming than like the genealogical work of Foucault. While such a list contains no single word capable of pinning down the nature of Rice's fiction with any degree of precision, the hope is that the heterogeneous, even contradictory nature of what follows, may collectively suggest something of the nature of Rice's mysterious polymorphous textuality, with its unsettling and ultimately unspeakable mixture of literary ingredients.

Citing the "origins" of fiction these days has become an increasingly problematic (some would say pointless) exercise. Postmodernist fiction writers and theorists have pretty much demolished the entire notion of authorial originality, emphasizing instead the ways that all literary works are ultimately the result of an endless chain of signifiers that have been continually modified, appropriated, plagiarized, and pirated. In this bizarre world, news concerning the "Death of the Author" is not greeted with grief but hailed as liberation from tyranny. Doug Rice, then, must *in deed* surely be the deadest of all authors—though this death paradoxically has resulted in some of the liveliest and most memorable, and vital fiction of any of his contemporaries.

Skin Prayer performs T.S. Eliot's notion that the entry of the new should have an affect on Tradition. His work is an extended example of a literary heritage associated with the writings of Artaud, Kristeva, Sarduy, Bataille, Faulkner, Aeschylus, Heraclitus, and most recently of saints and mystics. Rice's work can be situated in a lineage of visionary, incantatory rants, raves similar to those that Patti Smith retrofitted into wild Dionysian celebrations of excessive sensual pleasures. In her Babelogues, Smith would deliver, to delirious audiences, part poetic invocations, part denunciations, part orgiastic celebrations of sensual pleasure accompanied with blasphemous treatments of myths and icons revered by religion or politics. Rice's erotic appetites of irrationality are similar to the rants and chants of Patti Smith. Wild and disobedient bodies of desire.

Although it's impossible to pin down the exact source of Rice's origins (even his mother denies his origin), certainly one of the contributing factors is precisely the ways that Rice radically critiques the entire notion of the authorial "I" (and by extension, of ANY "I" presumed to be the stable, unified identity depicted in realism). Instead of unity, Rice gives us multiplicity—fictive texts emerging from other sources, other identities, other texts, and other personas.

Once in a bar in San Diego, Rice dared any of us to say bricolage without bleeding. "Your mouth should explode just in trying to say." Like Lenny Bruce's—"What do you mean *we* white boy?"—Rice challenges those ideological Romantic notions of the writer as genius. As an individual. The empty gestures of the lone ranger in a garret baring her or his soul. The silly and reductive mild manners of the cult of personality (I mean, cult of originality). The tortured artist rejected by family and friends and society. Rice is revolted by such posing. Disinherited writers condemned to wearing black and drinking coffee drinks that have everything in them but coffee. The writer cursed with *having to* write. On more than one occasion, even right here in *Skin Prayer,* Rice has invited friends to come on and be a Pepper, too! The ever-so sophisticated "cutting-edge fringe" that Rice repeatedly bemoans since the hip members of this group are not even aware of how they are "owned" and "manufactured" by the center. The ones who deny shopping malls[2] and television programs because they (the radical avant-garde [whatever that would be in an MTV world {it would be a television commercial of cours}]) are the ones who just cant get it. (Cant is correct. Don't mess with my words.) It does hold, Bill. It does. Rice, himself, however has been known to speak through two lips twice at once. The end result of such cannibal and viral languages is immediately evident throughout selections in *Skin Prayer*.

Reading *Skin Prayer* is akin to watching *Tetsuo Ironman* – the frantic energy pulling bits from the junkheap of history. (This thought just crossed my mind.)

Rice seeks the knots on the skin. Here.

And while there is no doubt that some of this multiplicity, the seeming ease with which Rice crosses and negotiates the drifting though of so many sorts of literary and psychological borders despite the wrenching emotional nature of such journeys, can be explained by Rice's deep emersion with the theory of critics like Deleuze and Guattari, Blanchot, Irigaray, Cixous, and Federman, who all stress the provisional nature of identity, perhaps an even more significant source of influence in this regard is Rice's background with the Jesuits and with Catholicism in general.

IV. The Art Of Taking A Walk

Like William S. Burroughs' work, it is useless to attempt to divide up Rice's writings into usual categories. I would argue that Rice's works collectively represent a single work. Thus, all

---

[2] If you have never gone to a mall with Doug Rice, you really need to do so. On more than one occasion, he has had to be escorted out of malls for performing sub-textual interventions and dialectical playfulness with the desires of Capitalism. Recently in Sacramento, Macy's downtown, there are rumors of a bra episode that is downright Wittgenstenian by nature.

Rice's writings—of whatever category we whish to assign them—proceed in that Burroughsian sort of manic feedback loop of self-reflexiveness, critical theory, and fiction. Everything happens all over all at once. Here to go.

Rice's fiction operates so strangely that its peculiar logic (radically different from the "realist" reliance on creating an illusion of causality, gradual revelation, epiphany) may make categorizing his writing an irrelevant or a hopeless task. Perhaps the latter is true but most certainly not the former. For Rice, himself, frequently introduces both the concept and numerous concrete examples of classification—and the resistance to the ways its precision holds in the world. Rice thus uses references to literary categories in many of his titles. Autobiography, prayers, litany appear in titles of texts that initially seem like safe, normalized literary categories. But in Rice's texts the certainty of stable genre categories collapses. The recurrence of traditional genres in titles of Rice's work indeed suggests their underlying homology, impulses unrelated to rhetoric so much as pointing to basic aspects of —not merely mockery but irony. An irony used as a kind of thin mask barely concealing the naked, bleeding, quivering, agonized truth just beneath the skin. In Rice's case, in fact, this becomes deeply and movingly autobiographical. His fragments of word-blood are made from memories burned so deeply inside the fleshly receptacle of his soul that the miraculous encodes them for later retrieval. But there is pain and at times devastation in such a turning back into the self and into the opening and peeling back of layers of skin to move to memory-desire. Rice's bone is touched, blackened, entered, after which come the marrow, the drive to understand a truth of some sort.

Thus, while doomed to failure, the following is a list of terms that might be used in the Sisyphean task of rolling a ball of terminology—or an entire apple cart containing several balls—

up the steep incline of Rice's genre-blending, discourse-crunching textuality. Such an effort is fraught with dangers, perils of terminology, that may eventually cause the apple cart to topple; its classificatory balls released to roll down the hill—at which point my readers are invited to join me in reversing our direction downwards and then beginning our collaborative laborious process anew, a process whose futility is in no way diminished by our the awareness that it is futile, for indeed, what other goal other than the futility of expression could possibly be worth this collaborative effort to scale such classificatory heights?

Skin Prayer can be described as:

—The ravings of a lunatic.
—A voice crying in the wilderness.
—Another installment in what amounts to a single, interminable, visionary novel (of nearly medieval epic proportions). It is a vast labyrinth of words that Rice has painstakingly rescued from their fallen status as mere building blocks in the enormous construction projects of lies and illusions being fashioned to support the trivial interests of commerce, politics, and literary realism. The intertextuality of Rice's mad writing (or his own aesthetic and psychological wiring) creates historical (if not hysterical) *friction*, not fiction. I have taken long walks with this Rice character. I have experienced his insane routines of behavior. The way he gathers words from the streets. The way he plays with passersby. Moving language bodies. (Don Harrold has told me stories of car rides. Long rides. The famous Barbie drive from Elmira, New York, to Salem, Ohio.)
—A violent and unforgiving textuality of flesh.
— A sequence of personal obsessions expressed in bruised and broken words. Rice attempts throughout *Skin Prayer* to re-

store these battered words that no longer cast a reflection in the mirror to their original connection with divine powers of creation and then fashion them into prayers, which unfold not via the usual fictional structures of plotted narrative, causality, character development, and epiphany but as a series of brief, chaotic, powerfully transgressive images. Stories emerge from out of nowhere as isolated (and isolating) fragments of narration. Rice denies. Rice refutes. Rice refuses the coherence of narrative. Rice's language pushes beyond deferral. Kristevean semiotics against the grain of his polytongual needs to become. His words are related only by their status as blasphemous expressions of the agony and violence of fleshly desire. These are desperate supplications and denunciations directed by a sinner to a very, very angry God. Rice gives us writing meant to relieve us from our unrelievable sense of guilt and from the curse of mortality that condemns us to oblivion for having committed sins. Sins that we were created to commit.

— An assemblage of prayers that Rice chants either to a room inside the prisonhouse of fleshly mortality which God has banished him to for having displeased Him (Rice's wrathful, all-powerful Father-God figure is always a "he") or to a woman who, like Beatrice, pulls him into the light of his own desire. Rice repeatedly is determined to manipulate God himself by deliberately opening himself up to God's desire and then by surviving a punishment he knows he deserves and accepts as a sinner in the brutally, rough hands of this angry God. *Skin Prayer,* thus, gives voice to an endless series of supplications, recriminations, pleas offered up not for the forgiveness God promised, but for a mystical moment in which all past and future disappears and consciousness suddenly unmoored from the process of becoming manages to escape from time itself into ecstatic contemplation of itself as a moment.

—A vast labyrinth built of words. The tradition and individual talent of many writers with diverse backgrounds have infected Rice. He extends the literary projects of numerous authors. Rice's "own" project may be thought of as an effort at self-creation, text-tending, and building upon some of the radical formal methods he developed in his two earlier books (*Blood of Mugwump* and *A Good Cunt-Boy Is Hard to Find*). *Skin Prayer* brings together historical and personal fragments from a guilt-ridden saint struggling to find a means of rediscovering divine power through the divinity of language, escaping from the prison cell of gender to which his characters have been mistakenly confined to for life without possibility of parole; *Skin Prayer* is the first major work of trranssexual fiction. Rice once told me that he wanted to fuck biological destiny. Really. I mean to fuck biological destiny.

—A book, which depicts the plight of gender in a postmodern world. *Skin Prayer* experiments with point of view and manages to voice the bewilderments and convulsions experienced by those liminal states of the body. Rice gives a powerful analysis of the peculiar instances in which members of one gender become convinced that they have been imprisoned in wrong gender expression. One of the Derridean "signature" elements of Rice's prose is the way that he obliterates borders of gender identity and voice. Rice's crazed, obsessive narrative depicting the longing to be a woman (at times his insistence that he "really" *is* a woman) replaces the physical unreality of his body.

—*Skin Prayer* represents one of the most compelling and original examples of transgressive fiction whose transgressions extend well beyond those quaint, safely quarantined forms of what passes for "bold and daring transgressive fiction" these days. The kind advertised by so many university presses.

—*Skin Prayer* seamlessly blends features of both the family novel and the rites of initiation novel into a wildly comic whole whose exaggerations become a singly, parodic, examination of the breakdown of the family, the psychological traumas inflicted on children reared in abusive, dsyfunctionality. Rice's willfully disconnected narrative and inconsistent presentation of characters, his refusal to present characters as much more than anything other than an assemblage of random quirks and verbal ticks, and an absence of denouncement or any sort of dramatic revelation in which the main character achieves knowledge or deeper awareness about himself or anything else become emblematic of a larger sense of skepticism and confusions characterizing contemporary American life. It is not so much that Rice rejects traditional forms of story-telling, as he stares ferociously, without blinking, at the naked moment. And writes past the readily available language into the reality of the naked lunch, the moment frozen on the spoon.

   —*Skin Prayer* is the most extended example yet of a fiction capable of modeling a repulsive force somewhat analogous to gravitation. Rice's prose is a seductive movement that accelerates a process of isolation and separation. One that suggests an eventual situation in which all words will be completely unable to communicate with any other, a time when information will cease circulating, and the universe of discourses will continue moving away from each other until even the memory of the warmth and security supplied by meaning and coherence will be only the distant memory of those doomed to experience an ever-increasing amount of darkness, isolation, separation, and incoherence.

> *"I was bruised and battered*
> *I couldn't tell what I felt*
> *I was unrecognizable to myself/*
> *I saw my reflection in the mirror*
> *I didn't know my own face."*
> —Bruce Springsteen

Although *Skin Prayer* will no doubt be published as a novel that can be read independently of Rice's other works. It actually is the third volume or installment of his version of *Death On The Installment Plan*. *Skin Prayer* is a single, massive experimental novel whose innovative and obsessive forms become Rice's primary means of self-expression.

Rice's work provides one of the most compelling indications yet that the reports being widely circulated about a whole series of deaths—of the author (and authority), of identity (at least the demise of the sort of stable, psychological based model of identity that has long been not only the staple of realistic fiction but the principle structural metaphor through which most westerners have conceived of themselves), and of realistic fiction as well as of vital, ambitious experimental fiction, have been greatly exaggerated. Likewise, its obvious vitality and capacity to amuse, confound, and otherwise engage readers also helps to render as instantly obsolete the series of obituary notices that have recently appeared sadly announcing the passing of reading and writing, even reality itself.

Despite its eschewal of plotted narrative, *Skin Prayer* remains a penetrating psychological portrait of the artist as a young flagellate, authored by a mysterious figure referred to as Douglas[3] or Doug Rice whose continuous contradictions, raving, obsessive and repetitious treatment of the same set of images and symbols relating to pain and instability to sustain an idea or to allow images to unfold gradually in coherent, chorographical ascension. This style of writing has the ironic effect of gradually producing a moving and utterly convincing series of Joycean epiphanies exploring the philosophy behind Acker's will "to suicide" that is unrivalled in its poetic intensity

---

[3] "While this name has numerous symbolic associations, it is most obviously a reference to one of his Father-figures, Douglas Springsteen

and analysis of body and language, or more apropos of body through language.

V. Why It's Hard To Be A Saint In The City

Rice startles readers with his original treatment of color imagery, perhaps influenced by Rimbaud's experiments in producing contexts in which words could be conjoined to associations and ideas in mysterious ways. Unspeakable ways. Particularly notable in this regard is the predominance of red (coupled with that of blue—Gass? Wittgenstein?). Red, which is traditionally associated with a narrative range of possibilities (red as passion, bodily), private (numerous references to a "red-haired woman"), literary (Acker, Burroughs, Joyce, Eliot), and historical (the red hair traditionally assigned to their most influential saint, Loyola),[4] dominates Rice's color schema.

Recursive fragments, highly charged with religious and personal resonance (natural images of the desert and rivers and the ocean, water and blood) lie all over the floor. Dead man talking. *Skin Prayer,* thus, is a collection of unattributed fragments of speech and writing which Rice has plundered in vari-

---

[4] For the historical and literary basis of the physical attributes traditionally assigned to Loyola (including his red hair color), see Jean Lacouture (3-4). Loyola was a latter day John the Baptist who founded the Jesuit Order that would eventually have such a dramatic and decisive impact on Rice and his alter egos after he was exposed to their philosophies during his troubled, early years. Like Joyce, this Jesuit institution shaped Rice's imagination. The Jesuit Order not only supplied Rice with a central vocabulary, set of icons and images that he would later pirate and recycle into blasphemous prose, but it was perhaps Loyola's famous and influential dictum—"Be all things to all men"—which most deeply infected Rice as a model, whose full implications he has explored more thoroughly than any other contemporary author.

ous pirated raids that yielded wealth whose treasures including everything from lengthy passages, individual images, motifs, symbols, sentences, right on down to character names and individual words—a bounty of literary plunder that Rice subsequently retrofitted into his fiction over which Rice proudly raised the flag of piracy thereby creating an audacious literary aesthetic whose reliance on the strategies of appropriation, pastiche, and plagiarism boldly announced a complete break from the traditions of authorial originality and uniqueness.

VI. The Form Of Prayer

Most fundamentally, the fictions in *Skin Prayer* can be best understood as being related to the form alluded to in the title; that is, as a work whose deepest affinities are with the prayer. In Rice's hands, prayer becomes a peculiar form of literary expression. Rice uses language as a conduit to God. Prayer becomes a literary form possessing its own rhetorical traditions, familiar icons and symbols, and mythic underpinnings, all of which are used by Rice to speak to God. And Rice creates this prayer out of skin.

One possible reading of Rice's use of the word *Prayer* is to simply highlight a kind of ironic narrative operation. That is, some readers may only look directly at the "content" of this work and immediately assume that *prayer* was being introduced here for mere and deliberately ironic purposes. And indeed, the "content" of Rice's *content* is indeed repellent—its sadomasochism, its constant figuring of God the father as a wrathful, irrational tyrant out to punish sinners, its equally transgressive treatment of sin, damnation, its repeated figuring of religious ecstasy in torrents of sadomasochistic images. Rice's "content" pushes at the boundaries. These major themes and motifs here include self-mutilation and flagellation, the relationship between eroticism and death, the violence and frenzy of sexual pleasure, the separation of the body and mind, the futility of any hope of achieving salvation, the irrelevance of reason as a means to understand our shared condition, the rampant subjective and delusional nature of sensory awareness, the ways that mankind is mired in a flesh-prison from which there is no means of ever reaching spiritual damnation or resurrection, the sinful nature of desire, the frenzy of sexual passion and/ of love as a sadomasochistic enterprise, the ecstasy of pain .seems to provide plenty of evidence, plenty of artillery with which to launch an all out attack on the filth sponsored by NEA that would put an end to its existence once and for all. Such readings are only obvious initially (obvious enough to have been the one that Senators Jesse Helms and John Ashcroft attempted to use as a weapon by citing Rice's earlier work, *Blood of Mugwump,* as being exactly the sort of sacrilegious, scurrilous, obscene art that congressmen can use as evidence for withdrawing the NEA-supported work).

The problem of such a reading, as with the analogous misreading of autobiography, far from mocking either the literary category or the elaborate system of Christian, especially Catholic, Beliefs responsible for the emergence of prayer as a codified literary form in the first place, is that Rice is dead serious (if playfully so) about this terminology. Above all what we are reading here is fundamentally and essentially a series of prayers, hymns, pleas for forgiveness, a style of supplication, an offering of or a recounting of Rice's sins which are acknowledged as sins and for which punishment is willingly accepted. These are expressions of flights of rapture in which the author uses words to try to satisfy God's judgment concerning his guilt and needed punishment. They are also expressions designed to move the consciousness responsible for their creation not only outside the Catholic systems of rewards and punishments but also to move toward lyrical flights into realms of unreason and the unspeakable. Rice's words are capable of literally lifting their creator out of the entire process of becoming.

Rice's narrators repeatedly long to be *here*, inside *this*, throughout the narratives collected in *Skin Prayer*.

(A fragmented digression moving toward an essay that is yet to be written.)

Some people pray
Some people play music
Bruce Springsteen

For Bruce Springsteen, this physicality of the religious experience is of the most literal kind—displays of athleticism, sheer-crazed exuberance, jumping into crowds, leaping over tall pianos and amplifiers in single bound. These physical displays are partly due to rock's usual masculine display, but as Springsteen revealed in his taped commentary appearing on the PBS rock music series, this physical display, including invitation to audiences, has its spiritual dimensions as well: "I always felt that if you can get the body moving, the spirit will follow, even, physical release, displays of sheer body until both performers and audiences feel they are completely spent and thus more receptive to the spirit."

Rice's presentation of the body is less literal, but no less grounded in an urge to force audiences into recognizing the fleshly origins of reading, writing, and artistic production and to force them to recognize their own imprisonment in fleshly states of physicality and cycles of birth, death, life. Rice brings us into the embodied awareness of the fleshly basis of sensation.

This division of labor that Springsteen seems to be positing between the raucous activity of playing music and religious people expressing their deepest longings and fears within a secular, religious activity is perhaps all very fine so long as it doesn't insist that this is an either/or proposition in which religious expression replaces rock and roll rather than a both/an expression. Actually Springsteen's lyrics make it very clear indeed that Springsteen has a considerably more complex view of things. He creates populist art seeking expression that satisfies physical exhilaration and uses rock to create a sense of transcendence, a visionary state of exhalation and of the physical, a sense of community that brings one closer to a higher power than is possible through the old-fashioned binary opposition.

These lines appear as part of a montage of images skillfully and vividly introduced that combine to create a composite portrait of human suffering, greed, a reliance on the illusion of hope and promise embodied in the America Dream that leads them out onto the endless roadway to personal oblivion, to disillusionment, loss of faith, and personal ruin. The evocation of Steinbeck's Tom Joad, the repeated, ghostly figure of defiance and protection, offers a helping hand to the brotherhood of workers who share the same values. By the end of the song, Joad never materializes. The listener may well wonder if he's just another pipedream offered by a system too canny to withhold all hope. A system that manufactures images so that the faith, necessary for maintaining stability, is now easily reified into mass produced images and then gladly purchased by a public for whom the effects of nostalgia and denial make them more than willing to not only naively accept these assurances but to shell out good money for their pleasures of having their own desires measured, marketed and then sold back to them on the marketplace.

Skin Prayer is a playful clue about what sort of work Rice intended to write—one, which is not so much a new direction for his career as it is a continuation of his own indeterminacy. A careful examination of the evolution of Springsteen's work reveals that at least since the release of his nightmarish descent into the murderous, bewildered condition of a particularly awful form of hell called loneliness and alienation, Sprinstgeen has increasingly and obsessively used sadomasochism, portrayals of men suffering eternal damnation for sins their ancestors committed, schizophrenia, the instability and insubstantiality of identity, the unknowability of anyone or anything, even oneself, and a stubborn faith, a devastating need born out of desperation. With Rice, Springsteen stands, throbbing, at the doorstep of an inability to face the truth about just how truly and deeply tragic human existence is. There at that door Rice confronts the difficulties of reconciling any notion of possible goodness or fairness to a supreme deity capable not only of imagining such a tragic state of introducing life into a universe but with a turn of the screw allowed, even ordained that life would evolve eventually into sentient beings who at some point in their development would be able to fully see death for what it was— after which, nothing else ever really mattered. Both Rice and Springsteen recognize the finality and the irrevocable nature of mortality, a condition that was not only dire but also hopeless— or at least was hopeless if reason and kinds of logic governing daily life were to hold, unless some outside power got introduced, relied upon. Springsteen used many of the same disturbing images and settings that Rice would later introduce in his fiction

("Between what's flesh and what's fantasy.")

Rice seeks hidden elements, subtleties concerning the struggle between body and spirit, and a presentation of language unrivaled by any of his contemporaries in terms of the hallucinatory vividness of the imagery, and physicality. Rice searches to uncover a literal, physical rendering of the act of speaking— and of the words and sentences that are propelled from inside the body-prison outwards into a sort of mysterious existence whose actual nature lies outside the categories used to process and make sense of any other source of sensation. Rice's writing turned into a muscle, a power that is almost intolerable in its sheer, brute, intensity and is certainly unrivaled by any of his contemporaries in terms of its immediacy and visceral haunting. "Larry, the muscle of word-making. Where words come. Where they breathe. The breathing of muscles coming near speech."

Doug Rice continues to be an author mercilessly ridiculing the outrageous and unpredictable treatment of identity. In all his work, he has mounted an assault on character/identity as a stable set of characteristics (the staple of realism's treatment). Simultaneously, he writes fiction so uniquely imagined that he can create a textual landscape whose haunting sense of personal violation, confusion, and spiritual longings is exceptional. Rice's work is outrageously personal and individualized and recognizably his own. He rigorously and humorously makes a mockery of the post-modern mockery his writing has grown out of and has been influenced by. Allegedly, that is.

As with small handfuls of other literary experimenters working on the fringes of academic and avant-pop guerrilla warfare on mainstream banality, Rice may well introduce theory in his writings as a shorthand means of pointing to certain tendencies in the craft of fiction an the art of living. It is equally apparent, however, that his treatment of point of view, gender confusion, character as disconnected fragments of broken words, disembodied body parts (particularly those associated with the physical act of speaking—the throat, the lips, mouth, the teeth) emerges so deeply and naturally out of the internal logic of his prose that citing "theory" as its source or to describe it is like using string theory to explain why a coin landed on tails a moment ago.

Most fundamental of all these shared affinities is the intuition that appears often to guide every movement in twisting labyrinth of his prose—a point perhaps most succinctly and forcefully made by Batille when he opens his discussion concerning the divine nature of eroticism, the religious meaning of eroticism, by noting casually, "The meaning of eroticism escapes anyone who cannot see its *religious* meaning." He goes on to clarify this notion in terms that almost seem to provide a gloss on what we encounter in Rice's work.

Refusing to settle his fiction upon realism's bedrock of plotted narrative and stable, psychologically-based presentation of character, Rice instead obsessively focuses instead on a "now"— a fleeting moment of consciousness existing in the impossibly narrow instance in which the past surges into the future. Whereas realism's emphasize on arranging materials into structure of rising action, development, climax, denouement has the affect of arranging sentences into web of connections, all elements subordinated to the climax, etc., Rice willfully severs these connections.

(There are rumors afloat in Paris and San Diego that Rice is about to take on Deleuze. Calling his bluff. The shoreline and the sea. Rice is currently writing a philosophical book called *Sacrificial Languages*. A book of literary theory about a woman's head on a pillow. A lock of hair. "An East coast book," Rice says. "One that will erase *Skin Prayer*, the force of becoming amnesia. A torn raincoat with writing under the sleeve. Get the message?" Recently in a telephone conversation, Rice told me he had found words that Deleuze didn't know about. The kinds of words that Deleuze could not recognize. "It's why he had to leap out that window, Larry. Ritual words written beneath stones and hidden sometime after midnight. Not blue words from *Dracula* that signify past desires, but words of water given from her skin. I know a woman who carries water, Larry.

A water carrier. Not an unnamed lover but a woman named at the threshold. Deleuze only approached the threshold. He came to the threshold. He could not step beyond the threshold. Into the moving through the threshold. Look more carefully into the mirror. Damn you. From behind. I gotta go, Larry. There's a wounded girl at my doorstep calling my name."

A few minutes later Rice called me back. "Listen to this, Larry." And he sang "When Doves Cry" to me. "See. I have figured something out. Cain was just a man. At one time I've got the wilderness. I'm done with this *Skin Prayer,* the whole idea. I'm writing this other book, *Thirty-three Stones of Passion.* …" Rice became disconnected due to technical problems that have been plaguing the phone lines at California State University Sacramento.)

More radically than any other author I am aware of. Rice fails to thrust (At first I, too, thought of this thrusting as just some sort of horrible typing error. I thought it had something to do with trust, but I think Larry has stumbled upon something other here.) his body. Only his language. The ties that bind.

Readers will be forced to acknowledge that there are many identities breaking apart Rice's skin. Rice is not any single individual but the most polymorphicaly perverse myriad in postmodern lit: Rice is a voice of bone, in bone, a masochist and a sadist of language and body, a sinner beneath the thumb of strong women and saints, a devoted father, a cunt boy forever, the most radical application of an ascetic whose obsessive search for spiritual succor has vowed to renounce completely his life as a sensual being, a perpetual wanderer in a post-modernist apocalypse version of Eliot's waste, a man seeking release from the imprisonment/hallucinations endured in the fleshly prison of maleness, a viral plague, a bruised and broken voice emerging from perpetual birth pangs whose inarticulateness can only come to color, the deep blue-purple color a pinch-mark. The sky becoming blue.

I wish God would send me a word/Something I'm afraid to lose.

—Springsteen, "Drive all Night"

In the end, (or perhaps through the beginning as we move through Rice's narrative), Doug Rice has come West. He is a crystallized, crazed energy, a passionate, deeply engaged teacher, one of those rare fiction writers whose voice and sensibility are uniquely his (her?) own (a paradox of course, given the fact that Rice is also one of the most daring appropriation artists working today, a writer whose works both mock the whole notion of originality and uniqueness even as Rice recontextualizes his stolen words within a new literary context immediately recognizable as becoming an authentic signature *of* Doug Rice, but not necessarily an authentic signature *by* Doug Rice.). Still, Rice remains signature. A making of ink. His language is as close to muscle as words can come. A raw rubbing into the tissue of the body. Rice's words are like St. John's feet, like Kurt Cobain's blisters, Patti Smith's throat. Here.

Doug Rice is also dangerously transgressive—"dangerous" in the most positive sense I can articulate—i.e., dangerous in that Doug Rice and his work will UPSET those they come in contact with; dangerous in the sense that those opening up their minds and mouths to be penetrated by Rice's word-virus will find the experience one of being violently pushed, shoved, probed, assaulted, off the familiar grooves that our lives and imaginations have carved out for us. Rice forces us to go beyond those structures that allow us to move effortlessly through the landscapes we travel on. His work jolts people off these grooves and that, as I say, is truly dangerous, because once you've been derailed you find yourself rumbling along into uncharted territories, never certain you will ever get back on track.

"Champagne, Champagne, a round for all the old choir-boys."

—"Bishop Danced," Bruce Springsteen

email from Larry in Idaho.

yo, "doug",

you've done a brilliant (and no doubt laborious)

job of cleaning up the mess i left behind and appear
to have even somehow managed to succeed with the
alchemist's dream: shit into gold. Seriously, this text
now seems to me to emerge out of the same crazed
darkness into a sort of light that SKIN does

the springsteen deletions were necessary (I will
develop these in the critifiction i will finish this fall
for my new book), and the occasional references
to him now seem to add a strange and often funny
perspective.

rather than change anything (no kidding, i really
love what is happening here!), let me suggest a
couple of minor additions:

….

There's also a very strange and relevant springsteen
lyric from "Mary Queen of Arkansas" that goes
something like:

You're not enough of a man to,? and ..."?? [sorry!
the lyric basically says something to the effect
that you aren't enough of a man to .... hate? and
not enough of a girl or woman to kiss

that would be cool to insert somewhere, if you can locate
it, but it's no biggie

doug, can't tell you how mnuchy i appreciate
what you've done for me here

hope to see you this weekend, will phone you
tomorrow nite when we get back from a trip
with lance and andi

bless you, my son,

larry

In the end, *Skin Prayer* is for:

My sister Dee Rice Schlotter
and
my friends Don Harrold and Leslie Heywood
who give me their time, their words, their love.
The ones who pulled me back to the shore.
Tugged me.
When I nearly slipped into the water.
For this.
The ones who insist I come home.

Doug Rice is the author of *Blood of Mugwump: A Tiresian Tale of Incest* (FC2/Black Ice Books) and *A Good Cuntboy is Hard to Find* (CPAOD Books). He is also a co-editor of *Federman: A to X-X-X-X* (San Diego State University Press). He has been the publisher and editor of *Nobodaddies: A Journal of Pirated Texts and Flesh* and is now beginning a new publishing house, Viral Publications. Currently, he is working on *Thunder Comes From This My House.* His work has appeared in numerous anthologies and journals. He teaches fiction writing at California State University

ERASERHEAD PRESS BOOKS
www.eraserheadpress.com

Eraserhead Press is a collective publishing organization with a mission to create a new genre for "bizarre" literature. A genre that brings together the neo-surrealists, the post-postmodernists, the literary punks, the magical realists, the masters of grotesque fantasy, the bastards of offbeat horror, and all other rebels of the written word. Together, these authors fight to tear down convention, explode from the underground, and create a new era in alternative literature. All the elements that make independent films "cult" films are displayed twice as wildly in this fiction series. Eraserhead Press strives to be your major source for bizarre/cult fiction.

MY DREAM DATE (RAPE) WITH KATHY ACKER
by Michael Hemmingson

In this new collection of fictions—a handful of small tales and two novellas—Michael Hemmingson retains his notorious status as the subversive prince of the avant-pop; or, as stated in The American Book Review, "one of the reckless youths of a quick and dirty literature."

Sex, drugs, Raymond Carver's ghost, Barbie dolls loving GI Joe dolls, the pure vaginas of French girls, the un-pure vagina of Kathy Acker, crack whores, nutty neighbors, scatological girlfriends, iniquitous fiends, Jesus freaks, pornographers, pushers, movers, shakers and winning lottery tickets are just some of the topics found in this unique book that is certain to titillate and aggravate the finest minds of the 21st Century.

ISBN: 0-9713572-9-3, 176 pages, trade paperback: $10.95 us

SOME THINGS ARE BETTER LEFT UNPLUGGED
by Vincent W. Sakowski.

A post-modern fantasy filled with anti-heroes and anti-climaxes. An allegorical tale, the story satirizes many of our everyday obsessions, including: the pursuit of wealth and materialism;the thirst for empty spectacles and violence; and climbing whatever social, political, or economical ladder is before us. Join the man and his Nemesis, the obese tabby, and a host of others for a nightmare roller coaster ride from realm to realm, microcosm to microcosm: The Carnival, The Fray, The Garden of Earthly Delights, and The Court of The Crimson Ey'd King. Pretentious gobbledygook or an unparalleled anti-epic of the surreal and absurd? Read on and find out.

ISBN: 0-9713572-2-6, 156 pages, trade paperback: $9.95

THE KAFKA EFFEKT
by D. Harlan Wilson
A collection of forty-four short stories loosely written in the vein of Franz Kafka, with more than a pinch of William S. Burroughs sprinkled on top. A manic depressive has a baby's bottom grafted onto his face; a hermaphrodite impregnates itself and gives birth to twins; a gaggle of professors find themselves trapped in a port-a-john and struggle to liberate their minds from the prison of reason—these are just a few of the precarious situations that the characters herein are forced to confront. The Kafka Effekt is a postmodern scream. Absurd, intelligent, funny and scatological, Wilson turns reality inside out and exposes it as a grotesque, nightmarish machine that is always-already processing the human subject, who struggles to break free from the machine, but who at the same time revels in its subjugation.
ISBN: 0-9713572-1-8, 216 pages, trade paperback: $13.95

SATAN BURGER
by Carlton Mellick III
A collage of absurd philosophies and dark surrealism, written and directed by Carlton Mellick III, starring a colorful cast of squatter punks on a journey to find their place in a world that doesn't want them anymore. Featuring: a city overrun with peoples from other dimensions, a narrator who sees his body from a third-person perspective, a man whose flesh is dead but his body parts are alive and running amok, an overweight messiah, the personal life of the Grim Reaper, lots of classy sex and violence, and a fast food restaurant owned by the devil himself. 2001, Approx. 236 min., Color, Hi-Fi Stereo, Rated R.
ISBN: 0-9713572-3-4, 236 pages, trade paperback: $14.95

SHALL WE GATHER AT THE GARDEN?
by Kevin L. Donihe
"It illuminates. It demonizes. It pulls the strings of the puppets controlling the strangest of passion plays within a corporate structure. Everyone, every thing is a target of Mr. Donihe's wit and off-kilter worldview . . . There are shades of Philip K. Dick's wonderfully inventive The Divine Invasion (minus the lurid pop singer), trading up Zen Buddhism for unconscious Gnosticism. Malachi manifests where Elijah would stand revealed; and the Roald Dahl-like midgets hold the pink laser beam shining into our hero's mind. Religion is lambasted under the scrutiny of Corporate money-crunchers, and nothing is what it seems." - From the introduction by Jeffrey A. Stadt
ISBN: 0-9713572-5-0, 244 pages, trade paperback: $14.95

www.ingramcontent.com/pod-product-compliance
Lightning Source LLC
Chambersburg PA
CBHW030516020726
47494CB00004B/1119